A Home Subscription! It's the easiest and most convenient way to get every one of the exciting Coventry Romance Novels! ...And you get 4 of them FREE!

You pay nothing extra for this convenience: there are no additional charges...you don't even pay for postage! Fill out and send us the handy coupon now. and we'll send you 4 exciting Coventry Romance novels absolutely FREE!

SEND NO MONEY, GET THESE
FOUR BOOKS FREE!

- - - - - - - - - - - - -

C0381

Lady Brandy

Claudette Williams

FAWCETT COVENTRY • NEW YORK

LADY BRANDY

Published by Fawcett Coventry Books, a unit of CBS
Publications, the Consumer Publishing Division of CBS Inc.

ISBN: 0-449-50165-5

Printed in the United States of America

First Fawcett Coventry printing: March 1981

10 9 8 7 6 5 4 3 2 1

Lady Brandy

ONE

Dark lashes fluttered against brightly flushed cheeks and then flashed with intense green fire. Sir Reginald's twenty-four years had not yet hardened him against such wiles. He took a step backwards.

"Lord . . . , you can't mean it, Brandy. Eh, but you do, and stap me if I give in to your whims, for I shan't and that's final!" Nervously Sir Reginald ran his hands through his fair Brutus curls and eyed his cousin warily.

She moved in for the kill. One slender white hand reached and took hold of his exquisitely cut blue lapel. The other hand slid up the blue superfine and found his cheek.

"Reggie . . . dearest . . . cousin, brother, friend, for indeed you are all these things to me. Could you say me nay in this hour? I need you, Reggie. . . . The truth of it is that *Lara* needs you!"

He blanched. Lara's name brought thoughts that quickened his heartbeat and stripped him of his pride. He took a rigid stance.

"That is hitting a man when he is down, Brandy, and well you know it. Your friend has caused me—"

"Fond memories," cut in Brandy hastily. "Your summer together in Brighton was a deliriously happy one."

He inclined his head. "So it was . . . but *I* foolishly believed that . . . that Lara cared. However, she would have none of me. I remember well how quickly she departed at summer's end." His voice trailed off, and he moved away from his cousin. He paced a moment in the brightly furnished gold-and-brown drawing room of his mother's town house, coming to take up a stand by the window overlooking the quiet of Duke Street. His hands went behind his back and clasped one another, his eyes looked on the park before him but saw instead gentle blue eyes, softly curling yellow hair. He felt himself wince.

Brandy took a step toward him. What could she say that she had not already said before? There was no explaining her friend's odd behavior. She threw a wayward glowing red tress over her shoulder. Lara had formed a tendre for Reggie, it was something she had been quite sure of . . . but then . . . why bid him goodbye the way she had done? And now . . . her latest letter shrouded in mystery, full with words and saying nothing. What had gone wrong?

10

"Reggie, I am convinced that Lara is in some sort of trouble," she said at length.

He turned to view her. "Why?"

"I don't know why. I only know that more than her father's death was at the heart of her return. . . ."

"She said she wanted to break all ties with me . . . wouldn't marry me. . . ." His voice was scarcely audible.

"Yes, that's right, she said that, and when she said it her heart was breaking. Don't you see, there must be something we don't know . . . something she is afraid of. Reggie, she has been gone one month and only one letter . . . and that one is scarcely comprehensible."

He paced to and fro. "I don't want to run her to earth, Brandy. I don't want to press myself on her. I told her I would not do that."

"I am not asking you to renew your suit, Reg. I am merely asking you to accompany me to Quendon Abbey. I want to see her for myself, and you know Aunt will not allow me to travel with only my maid in attendance. It is too long a distance."

"You are asking too much of me," he said stubbornly, but already he felt his will weakening. His cousin had ruled his life ever since they had been children. Her coming of age some three years ago had only served to strengthen her power over him. He was her senior, but she had always presided over their games, and indeed it was as she had said, he was her cousin, her brother, her friend. It was hard to refuse her anything she so strongly desired. He attempted to back away. "At any rate,

11

it's only your imagination running off with you again, Brandy. . . ."

She put up her chin. "Was it my imagination when I told you we were being followed home the other night from Lady Sefton's? No, it was not. I was right. If we hadn't veered off into the alley and thrown our cloaks over—"

"Good gosh, Brandy . . . after all, it was only Fisk and Rally up to their tricks."

"Yes, but it could have been thieves, and the point is that I was right and I am right now! Lara is in trouble, and if you don't help I shall think very poorly of you, Sir Reginald!"

He shifted uneasily. He sensed that she had won the battle, but still he attempted a recovery. "You've got yourself all worked up over nothing, Brandy. After all, you have nothing solid to base your fears on."

She shoved Lara's letter into his hands and felt him tremble as he took it up. It touched her heart, and therefore she tempered her words.

"Reggie . . . you and I both know how placid, how reasonable, how gentle Lara is. Read this lamentable epistle and tell me if it is the same girl. Go on . . . just see how she rambles . . . and then there is that passage about her brother. . . ."

The drawing-room doors opened wide to admit Lady Anne, Sir Reginald's mother and Brandice Fernwood's maternal aunt. Brandy's eyes indicated caution as she glanced at her cousin and went forward to take up her aunt's hands.

Lady Anne was a tall woman whose fair locks had blended into soft waves of white silk which she wore cropped close to her lovely face. Her sweetness of disposition and strength of character were often displayed in her lively blue eyes. Her kindness had seen her niece Brandice through her youth, after Brandice's parents had been killed in a carriage accident. She was immediately intrigued by the warning look her niece sent her son. She put her hand into Brandy's and smiled warmly.

"Well, children . . . what are you at?"

Brandy sat beside her aunt on the gold damask sofa and turned to look full into her face. "You will not like it, Auntie, for I know you want me to enter the season, make a match, and settle down. And so I shall try and do, but first . . . first there is something I find I must attend to . . . an obligation, if you will. . . ."

Lady Anne put up her hand. "Make yourself easy, child, and tell me what all this frenzy is about."

Her son looked on uneasily. His mother's sweetness of nature concealed an iron will. He might find himself in disfavor with her after Brandy's recital, and this was something he was ever at pains to avoid. "Yes, I wish you would tell her that it is frenzy, and then perhaps we might be at peace again."

Lady Anne's blue eyes scanned her son and her brow went up. There was a weakness of character in the lad that she wished erased. "Reggie, why don't we allow Brandy to tell us what it is she wants before we pass judgment?"

He bit his lip and moved to the fireplace, where he took up a log and thrust it into the grate.

Women! They were all a pack of mysterious creatures full of whims and moods. A man never knew where he stood with any of 'em!

Brandy took a great inhalation of air and fixed her green eyes on her aunt's face. "Auntie . . . you remember my friend Lara. . . ."

"How could I not when she was with us all summer in Brighton?" returned her aunt gently.

"Yes, yes, of course." Her aunt had the knack of reducing her to the schoolroom. It was most vexatious when she wanted to appear as she was, quite grown, for indeed she was one and twenty! She tried again. "The thing is, Auntie, that Lara had to return home, as you know, when her father died suddenly."

"Yes?"

"Yes, well . . . I had not heard from her until this letter arrived yesterday. It is a very odd letter . . . written in her hand, but not like Lara at all."

"Your point, dear?"

"I suppose I simply want to visit with her and see for myself that she is well—that she has not been too dreadfully affected by her father's death. You see . . . we had such plans for the season. She was to stay with her cousin in Berkeley Square. . . ."

"But my dear, she may feel it is too soon after her father's death. Perhaps she will renew her plans when more time has passed."

"I realize that. Auntie . . . what I want is to visit with her at Quendon Abbey in the Cotswolds," she blurted out at last.

Lady Anne said nothing to this at first. It flitted through her mind that Brandice was more her

14

mother every day. She had been out for three seasons. Her beauty had dubbed her a 'diamond of the first stare'; her lineage and her fortune were enough to achieve her an enviable match, and indeed her offers were such as to thrill a matchmaker's heart. Yet she had taken to none, seemed to like her single state, and appeared determined to pursue her single career. It was unthinkable. The child was one and twenty. It was time she was settled. And then Anne thought of her own youth. She smiled to herself as she remembered how she too had been nearly two and twenty and denying every suitor that came to call ... ah, but then came Sir Reginald's father, and all had been lost.

"It is not the time for you to be undertaking a journey of that sort," she said gently.

"There can be no objection, Auntie, if Reggie escorts me ... ?"

Sir Reginald began to bluster out his refusal, then discovered his cousin's green eyes and somehow the refusal died in his throat. Her eyes spelled out a name: Lara, Lara, Lara. How could he deny himself this opportunity?

Lady Anne contemplated this. "My son's escort might be misconstrued by those forever looking for a piece of meat to chew."

"I don't understand," returned Brandy, puzzled.

"You see ... you are quite a beauty, my dear, and my son is unattached. It might be thought a ploy to ... force your hand into Reggie's."

"Oh! How horrid." She went from a dark frown into a bright gleam. "But that can be settled. We shall make Fisk accompany us."

15

Sir Reginald grinned. "Fisk go to the Cotswolds, *now*, when the season is upon us? I doubt that!" he scoffed good-naturedly.

Brandy put up her chin, "Leave Fisk to me, Reggie, and see if he don't come!" She turned to her aunt. "Well, then, if Reggie and Fisk accompany me . . . ?"

"You will go in the coach with a proper retinue. No riding horseback over the countryside," Lady Anne warned sternly.

Brandy laughed, excited with the prospect of the adventure.

"I promise."

"One month, no more. I expect you back in a month's time of your leaving!"

"Yes, yes, yes," cried Brandice Fernwood, putting her arms about her aunt and flying to the drawing-room doors. "I shall go and pack immediately." She turned and stopped a moment to give her cousin a bolstering look. "You won't regret it, Reggie, I just know that you won't!" With this she was gone, leaving both cousin and aunt to wonder how far from the truth this really was.

TWO

Lara scanned her young brother's face. Where had his color flown? His yellow hair lacked its usual luster, his blue eyes were dull, distant. She dealt the cards across the polished oak table of the schoolroom and wondered why the depression he had suffered over his father's death was taking such a toll.

"Denny . . . what is it? Don't you want to play at cards? Would you rather we went for a walk?" Lara asked gently, touching his hand. He was eleven years old. He should be running about, getting into mischief, putting the house into an uproar with his pranks.

He brought up his quiet blue eyes and scanned her face. His stomach churned. Something was wrong, but when the doctor had examined him he had said it was only sore spirits due to his father's

17

death. Why then did his stomach churn? Why didn't Lara make it better?

"Lara . . . I want Marden," He said in a little boy's voice.

She was moved to exasperation. Kurt Marden. Here was his name again. She didn't trust Lord Marden. Why did Denny want him? Her answer when it came was on a rough tone. "Denny, I have sent for him, but I am told he is away from home. However, as soon as he returns I am certain he will stop by."

The schoolroom door opened and a tall wiry gentleman dressed in country buckskin coat and breeches entered the room. A warm smile spread across his weathered features as Lara rose and went to greet him. She sighed in some gratitude, for there was something dependable about her cousin Alistair Hayward.

"Alistair . . . how good of you to come. . . ."

She was lovely. Soft and warm. He could, if she allowed it, grow to love her, but now it was important that she need him. He touched her cheek and felt pleased enough to see the color rush there. "Lara . . . I hear our young man is a bit under the weather?" He looked towards Denny.

Lara turned to her brother and frowned. The boy should have risen and made his greeting. "Denny, here is Alistair to bear you company." She urged a smile from him.

"Hallo, Hayward . . . good of you to come," said the child in adult fashion. He turned to his sister. "May I be excused, Lara?"

She frowned and felt her heart constrict. What

18

could she do? Why had her world turned upside down? "Yes, Denny. . . . If you are going to lie down and rest, take a book with you."

"Yes, Lara." Quietly he left the room, went to his own quarters, took up his basin, and disgorged what little he had eaten that morning. This done, he sighed. Nothing was staying down any more. He took up a wet linen, put it to his head, and sat on the edge of his bed. Was he dying as his father had done?

Lady Anne's favorite traveling coach rumbled over the scabrous roads. Brandy's aunt had insisted on her traveling in the massive chocolate-brown carriage with its gold satin upholstery, saying that she would have her niece travel in style. She twinkled as Brandy's nose crinkled up, for she was well aware that her notion of style and her niece's were far apart. However, Brandy knew well when to comply without argument.

John, one of Lady Anne's drivers wielded the reins of the double team, and beside him Sir Reginald's groom blew a cloud of trailing smoke from a pipe he had constructed himself. Behind them a neat pile of luggage was secured to the coach.

Within the well-sprung carriage Brandy attempted to disintegrate her restlessness in lively conversation with her young maid, Francy, who was naughty and full of idle chatter. Their common denominator was youth and the normal interest their respective situations gave them in men.

Without rode Sir Reggie and his friend the Honourable William Fiskinton, better known to his intimates simply as Fisk. Once Brandy had requested his company on this adventure there was never any question that he would come. He considered himself the first and the most valued of her suitors.

Three days' traveling had put them in the vicinity of Quendon Falls in the Cotswolds. This was supposed to deliver up their destination, Quendon Abbey. However, explicit directions from the villagers had served to turn a twenty-minute ride to the Abbey into a two-hour circle. Brandy's party found themselves momentarily in a quandary.

The coach and its accompanying outriders came to a complete halt beside a suspiciously familiar fingerpost.

Sir Reginald's groom, Abe, sucked on the stem of his pipe and then pointed it at the sign. "Eh, John, lookee where ye brought us! Told ye to turn off left. Wouldn't listen to me, would ye? No. Stubborn ye be."

"Stubble it! That weren't the right road."

Fisk moved his top hat forward and back over his auburn curls. His light-brown eyes scanned their surroundings thoughtfully.

"Plague take it, Reg . . . we've been this road before!"

Nettled, tired, and bad-tempered, Sir Reginald returned testily, "Why, Fisk, you are needle-witted! Of course we've been this road before. Abe is right, we should have taken that left!"

"No we shouldn't have!" retorted Fisk, firing

up. "Dirt road. It was a dirt road. The Abbey wouldn't be off a dirt road . . . egad . . . would it?"

In some exasperation Brandy plopped her blue silk top hat onto her carefully arranged copper cluster of long curls, buttoned up the blue silk spencer to her neck, ruffled her lace collar and cuffs, and jumped nimbly out of the carriage. "Now," she said getting the attention of the assembled company, "Abe, you will be so kind as to saddle my mare. I suppose I'll have to use my sidesaddle, dressed as I am . . . and perhaps *I* can lead us to the Abbey!"

Francy stuck her head out of the window, her marshy brown eyes wide with trepidation. "No, miss . . . ye promised her ladyship ye wouldn't go riding about on the open road while we be traveling."

"Hush now, Francy. I have no desire to drive about in circles all day when the Abbey must be very close by. I cannot see well enough from within the coach, and as I spent a short holiday with Lara at the Abbey some years ago, I fancy I might be able to recognize the correct turnoff." She turned to receive the reins of her bay mare as Reggie's groom tightened the girth.

A moment later she was mounted and leading the group off down the main pike. It felt good to be on horseback again, though she preferred to ride astride.

Fisk and Reggie urged their tired geldings forward to catch up to her as Fisk called out an entreaty. "I say . . . Brandy . . ."

She turned and giggled and urged her horse

21

into a canter, losing sight of them just around the bend. The trees were glorious in the start of their autumn splendor. Green was still dominant, but everywhere the woods were flecked with deep golds and rushes of peachy red. The road swirled upwards in its climb when she did in fact espy a familiar pattern. Marden Towers. Its brick walls and black iron gate with its seal of shiny gold glittered before her. The Marden Estates ran for some distance beside the lands of Quendon Abbey, but unlike the Towers the Abbey's gate was set back from the road by two hundred yards. They had simply just missed it!

She pulled up her mare, cooing to the horse, "There now, sweet mare ... Brown Sugar ..." For the mare was prancing in place, ready now for some action and perturbed at being held back.

She waited for her party to catch up to her and triumphantly pointed the way. "You see," she cried merrily, "what you needed was a woman in command." With this she gurgled and sent her mare forward and again left them to follow. This time they were torn between chagrin and relief.

Lara glided across the marble floor her father had installed in the great hall during his reign. Lord Marden noted that she looked well enough, considering the ordeal she had been put through these last few weeks. Her fashionable gown of ivory muslin had been made for her during her stay in Brighton, and it was evident now that she had lost some weight since then. A trim girl to

22

begin with, this weight loss gave her a haunted look. He bent over her hand and brushed it lightly with his kiss.

"Miss Quendon . . ." When he came up he noted that she looked nothing like her mother, if one went past the fair hair and blue eyes. No, Lara was very different. "I received your note and came as quickly as I could."

"You are too kind," she answered quietly and felt the old resentment churn. Her mother had been gone now five years . . . but still she could remember the bitterness. She wondered what Kurt Marden felt.

"Shall I go up to Denny's room?" He was impatient with her air of coolness. He had as much reason, if not more, to feel bitter, to feel resentment. He was moved momentarily with contempt.

She observed the flitting emotions pass through his eyes, but she did not understand them. Denny wanted him; well, then, let him go up. "Yes, why don't you. . . ."

He inclined his head. "I fancy I know the way, so you needn't bother taking me up," he said, and then he was gone.

She watched his departure, watched him take the stairs. He was nine and twenty and sought after by every matchmaking mother from Quendon to London. It was not a surprising thing. He was handsome, tall, broad, haut-ton, wealthy, and titled. He was also arrogant, self-assured, selfish, and a wanton libertine . . . or so it was said.

Her father had hoped for a match between them, but her mother had been horrified at the notion.

23

Even barring her parent's will she had never felt anything in that direction. It was not until she met Sir Reginald that marriage seemed an attractive prospect. Her parents had not been happy together, and she wanted something different. Sir Reginald. He was everything she had ever dreamed of in a man. And then her father had died . . . the letter from her aunt Cynthia, warning about her mother . . . about Denny. All question of marriage to Sir Reginald was cut at the heart.

She stood in the central hall surrounded by the paintings of her ancestors. Her brother was lord and master of the Abbey and all its holdings. Her brother was her responsibility . . . and she had allowed that man to go up to him alone. . . .

Brandy's cortege stopped with her to take in their surroundings. All were in awe of the eight-hundred-year-old building that stretched in grace before them. Gothic, wondrous, it stood a remnant of its past. Its extreme west front had surrendered to erosion and time, but despite these depredations, the quality of the stone carvings was still evident.

Brandy had the advantage of them, for she had spent time with Lara at the Abbey some three years before and knew something of its history. She began pointing out some of the Abbey's historical features. "And there to the north, Fisk, is the crypt."

"Don't like crypts."

They laughed and moved up the drive to the great front double doors, where they left their servants in charge of their equipage and live-stock.

Lara had one ivory-shod foot on the stairs ready to ascend and join Lord Marden in Denny's room when the great knocker reverberated the air with its heavy clanking. She turned and waited as Jeffreys, the Quendon butler, moved across the marbled floor and opened one of the double doors.

"Lara!" cried Brandice joyfully, rushing across the hall to fill the house with an air of excitement.

"Brandy . . . dearest . . . you are here. You are really here." And Lara embraced her friend.

Sir Reginald stood rigidly throughout this scene. Here was Lara. Soft, lovely, sad . . . there was something so very sad about her. He felt himself shake as he moved forward. What would he say? He had thought about this first meeting, after their last . . . and he still did not know what he could say.

Fisk discovered a rather large statue of a gargoyle under his gloved hand and jumped away from it. He found his surroundings just as he had expected. Cold, forbidding, and hinting of ghosts.

Brandy spoke. "I couldn't stay away, Lara. I hope you don't mind my descending on you without any notice. . . ."

Lara's hands took up the kid-gloved hands of her friend.

"Mind? Oh, Brandy . . . you are just what I need to set everything into its proper place."

Brandy stood aside, and her green eyes twinkled. "I have brought these two sad rogues. I know

25

you will forgive me, Lara, for I had no choice. Lady Anne would not let me tackle the open road without ample protection. But you needn't put them up here. I am certain they will be comfortable in the village inn."

Lara's blue eyes met Sir Reginald's. She allowed him to take up her hand and felt her entire body tremble.

"It is good . . . to see you again, Sir Reginald." She turned to allow Fisk to bow over the same extremity, though Sir Reginald gave it up reluctantly and Fisk did in fact have to pry it loose from his friend's grip. She smiled warmly at her friend when this was done. "What nonsense is this about the inn? Fisk and Reggie will stay here. We have ample room at the Abbey."

Fisk had discovered by that time an interesting portrait of one of the Abbey's inhabitants. The eyes of the monk seemed to him most ominous, and the longer he stared, the more he became convinced that this was not the place for a holiday. "Don't mind," he put in hastily. "I'll go to the inn . . . don't wish to put you out . . ."

"It's no trouble at all," Lara was saying.

Brandy heard her friend turn to the butler and say something about preparing rooms, but she wasn't really interested, for a movement on the main staircase caught her attention. Her bright-green eyes widened with appreciation and surprise. Here was the best-looking man she had ever seen. It was her first discernible thought. Blue-black hair gleamed as it waved in careless fashion over his brow, against his ears, near his neck.

Rugged, so rugged were his good looks. Tanned was his face, his jaw strong, his nose aquiline. His aqua-blue eyes twinkled. Laughing! Still she pursued her survey. His shoulders broad enough to match his height and his country buckskin denoted to Brandy's experienced eye a tailor of the first stare. She took in a little breath and cautioned herself. His type was often dangerous. Rakes they were. Conceited they were. Careful, now.

Tall and confident, he was quick to recognize her appraisal and returned one in kind. She noted this at once and laughed out loud. He grinned. Interesting, this copper-haired chit. Who was she?

Her laugh had drawn attention his way, so that he quickly completed the remaining stairs and was made known to them by Lara, who made polite—only polite—introductions.

Fisk and Reggie interrupted the introductions and astounded both Laura and Brandy by going forward and each taking one of Marden's hands and slapping his shoulder amicably.

"You dog, Marden! Evading the Jersey, eh? You were due back in London last week, she told us. Had it from Byron, who said you had finished with the Cotswolds and—"

Marden laughed and put up his hand. "Acquit me. I never wrote Byron. 'Twas Moore who swore I'd be back. Good lord, man, I have estates that need tending."

"Yes, but you've missed enough of Almack's, let me tell you. Jersey will cut you dead when next you attempt to enter those portals." Sir Reginald wagged a finger and grinned broadly.

"Come to dinner tonight." Marden extended his invitation to all, lingering the fraction of a second on Brandy's face. "And I might attempt to properly defend myself."

Lara shot him a look of disapproval. "My lord, it is my wish to entertain my guests in my home tonight. However, you are welcome to join us." It was obvious that he was not at all welcome.

He sobered. "I regret, ma'am, that I have a friend already promised to me this evening and would not impose on you to extend your invitation to him as well."

Fisk and Sir Reginald both turned to Lara, for it was evident that they wished Marden part of their set. However, she made no move to assure Marden that his friend was also welcome. A moment later Lara attempted to dispel the sudden tenseness. She moved away and threw up her hands with a short apologetic laugh.

"But where are my manners? Come, let us retire to the library, where we may be comfortable before the fire and have refreshments." She turned to Marden, "Do you join us, my lord?"

He could see that she did not wish him to do so, and perversity urged him to stay, but he had business awaiting him at the Towers, so he declined quietly and withdrew.

All this was not lost on Brandy. Why didn't Lara like him? For it was obvious that Lara did not. And he? He certainly took the snub well. Hard-cored, probably, inured to slights by the fact that he had to live with his wild reputation, if his looks were any indication. No doubt he had behaved improperly to Lara, and Lara had ever been a prude.

Happily did Brandy follow her friend into the library, where she noticed at once the portrait of the present lord. It had been in progress three years ago when she was last at the Abbey. He looked bright, full of mischief, and eager to be off. Such was his expression in the portrait.

"Oh, look . . . 'tis Denny!" cried Brandy sweetly and then turned to her friend. "Where is the young madcap anyway?"

Lara's smile vanished. "Denny has not been well. He is resting abovestairs."

Brandy's eyes grew grave. "Ah, Lara . . . so that was what you meant in your letter. What does the doctor say?"

"Nothing . . . just that he thinks it is his depression over papa's death. They were close, very close, you see."

"Depression, eh?" Fisk shook his head. "Not natural . . . for a lad, I mean. At least it wouldn't keep him abed . . . would it?"

Sir Reginald frowned his friend down and took a step towards Lara. "And you? How have you been?"

Suddenly she collapsed. The strain of worry heaved itself up and she fell in sobs against Sir Reginald's chest. He took her to him, petting, soothing with soft words.

Brandy and Fisk exchanged glances, and Fisk whispered that he thought he would just hobble down to the village inn. She stayed him with a firm grip. It was at this juncture that the library door was opened and in its wide painted frame stood a tall brunette whose middle age was scarcely detectable she was so attractive.

Lara sensed the woman's presence and immediately pulled out of Sir Reginald's comforting embrace. She sniffed, collected herself, and said quietly, "Aunt Cynthia . . . I am pleased to present my friends to you."

THREE

Cynthia Hayward's lush velvet trappings moved sensually to her walk as she entered the large darkly furnished room. The firelight, the dim gray light of descending dusk outdoors, the total mood of a promising night exactly suited her. However, she was not pleased by the sudden entrance of these people into her world. She smiled and hid her displeasure well, taking Sir Reginald to one side with her and placing her hand on his arm until she was escorted to the seating of her choice, this being an overly large gothic carving from where she was able to feel a sense of command.

She folded her hands in the lap of her cream velvet gown and smiled at the assembled group. "Now . . . what brings you to Quendon Abbey, and for how long may we expect to have the pleasure of your company?"

Brandy was amused by the woman. She knew something of Lara's Aunt Cynthia, for Lara had spoken of her many times, and never with affection. She answered her easily, "Lara brings us. We wanted to visit with her . . . extend our condolences to the entire family," she added as an afterthought and was surprised by Cynthia's reaction, "and attempt to bring Denny out of the dismals."

"Oh? I wasn't aware that you and Denny were acquainted," returned Cynthia, attempting to cool her words, for already she sensed that this girl, Brandice Fernwood, would be much in the way.

"Well . . . you were not here three years ago . . . but Denny and I were quite good friends," answered Brandy easily.

A tea tray with biscuits was brought in, and conversation scattered into idleness while the consumption of this repast was accomplished. Afterwards Lara came to the rescue by suggesting she show them to their rooms, where they might be comfortable after their long journey.

Once well away from the library, Brandy took up her friend's arm. "Whew, she is a tigress, isn't she?"

"Good-looking woman, your aunt," said Fisk in the way of conversation. There was much here that he did not understand, but more than that, that he wanted heartily to stay out of. Instinct was already waving a warning finger.

"Yes indeed," agreed Brandy, "she is good-looking . . . but cold."

Lara looked uneasy. "Denny doesn't like her . . . but that is because she is so managing."

"Speaking of Denny, just which is his room? I'll have a look in on him later," said Brandy.

" 'Tis the same . . . off the schoolroom. At the far end of the hall." She sighed. "I'll let you go in and refresh yourself now, Brandy . . . but later you must sit and keep me company, and we will talk."

"Yes, indeed we shall." She saw Lara lead Sir Reginald and Fisk off to their rooms and entered the brightly furnished yellow room with its huge four-poster bed. It was much the same as it had been when she had used it three years before. Lord, but it did seem a lifetime ago. So much had happened . . . three seasons, and here she was again, still a maid!

As it turned out Brandy did not have to go to Denny. He went to her. All he needed to hear was that Brandy was visiting with them. Immediately his spirits soared. He had formed a strong attachment to her during her visit, and though he had been only a child he had not forgotten the copper hair, the laughing green eyes, and the warmth.

A knock sounded at her door, and Brandy turned the book she was reading onto her bed and moved across the room, "Yes?"

" 'Tis Denny," said the lad softly.

"Why, Denny!" cried Brandy as she opened the door wide and took him to her in a gentle hug. "Good gracious, madcap, you have taken on some height, haven't you?" He grinned and stepped into her room.

She closed the door and turned to join him, and then saw his face full in the afternoon light. So great was her shock that she nearly gasped. Instead she maintained her composure and said on a grave note, "Now, Denny . . . what is this?" So saying she took up his chin, tilting it to her. His face was white, far too white. There was a dryness about his skin . . . a scaling near the hairline. He was thin, drawn, and not the robust lad his youth had promised.

He shrugged his shoulders. "I dunno."

She took up his hand and led him to a window table set, where she firmly sat him down and pulled up her own chair beside him.

"Let's talk."

"About what?" He wasn't looking at her. Irrationally he seemed ashamed of his ill health.

"Many things. Returning to Eton, for one."

He brightened. "That is what I want to do."

"Then, my lad, why haven't you?"

He sulked. "Aunt Cynthia told Lara I must observe the first month of mourning . . . and she was right. But then I went and got sick . . . and now they won't let me go till I get better."

"Aha! Well then, Denny, we must see about your getting better," said Brandy brightly.

He looked up at her quickly, and there was a fear in his blue eyes that communicated itself to her, "Brandy . . . what . . . what if I don't? What if . . . if I get really sick, like my father . . . and . . ."

"Stop it!" she commanded. "What we need to do is ply you with the right foods."

"I can't hold 'em," he complained petulantly.

34

She had been holding his small white hand when the Georgian diamond ring she always wore pricked the tip of his finger. She apologized lightly.

"Eh? Oh . . . I didn't feel it," he answered absently.

The scratch it left was barely visible and only a drop of blood oozed, but Brandy frowned and examined his hand. Her brow went up, for on his fingernails were transverse white lines. She pinched his fingertips.

"Do you feel that, Denny?"

He shook his head. "No . . ."

For no reason at all Brandy felt a chill sweep through her. This was no depression. The lad was seriously ill, and why the devil hadn't the doctor noticed? There was something about Denny's condition that triggered her memory, but her recall was out of focus. There was something about his appearance, something about his fingernail condition, that reminded her of something, but she knew not what this something was. She shrugged it off, stood up, and led him towards her door. He grinned wide, for she had a mischievous twinkle in her eyes.

"Where are we going, Brandy?"

"Below, to the kitchens, where, my lad, I shall make for you with m'own hands something you will hold down with pleasurable delight!"

He beamed happily. Even at his age he knew well enough that ladies of quality did *not* go into the kitchens and trouble themselves with the preparation of food. This was bound to cause something of a stir below, but it would not be the first time Brandy had caused a stir in his household, and he was thoroughly enchanted.

Deana Hopkins nodded to Jeffreys as she entered the great hall and slipped out of her dark-blue redingote and matching bonnet. It had been a tedious drive into town, but her Aunt Cynthia had always to be "pleased," especially since Deana had good cause to desire her aunt's approbation. Easy laughter, a woman's light musical laughter, brought her head up sharply, and with some agitation she witnessed Denny in the company of a young and far too beautiful maid just about her own age.

Brandy's laughter eased as she discovered a tall, dark-haired and not unattractive full-bodied girl. The girl's dress was neat, pretty enough but well worn. A moment later Deana was coming towards them clucking her tongue.

"Denny . . . what are you doing up? Your sister said that you would rest today." Reproachfully she glanced from the boy in short pants to Brandy's thoughtful countenance.

Denny took umbrage. He might be ill, but he wasn't going to be ordered about by this woman, and so he would show her! He put up his chin. "Deana . . . I should like to make known to you my very good friend, Miss Brandice Fernwood. She will be staying with us at the Abbey for a time." He turned in an aside to Brandy. "Deana Hopkins. We are connected through my Aunt Cynthia. Miss Hopkins is her niece." Then in a lower voice that was perfectly detectable to all present, "Deana's in the suds, you know . . . dun territory . . . been drying out at Quendon since July."

Miss Hopkins flushed angrily over his reference to her poor financial condition. She would have snapped his head off had she not the ability to cool her temper whenever her long-term plans called for it.

It was, however, obvious to Brandy that Miss Hopkins was collecting herself. Why? Denny had been cruel, and Brandy rather thought it was contrived. He didn't like Miss Hopkins and he made no attempt to conceal it. "Denny," said Brandy reproachfully but in a soft voice. Then she turned to Deana and said warmly enough, "How do you do? I am very pleased to make your acquaintance. I am also a friend of Lara's . . . and find myself at a loss, for I don't think she mentioned you when she spent the summer with us."

"Oh, yes . . . well, Lara and I had never met, you see. I arrived here shortly after she left to stay with you in Brighton," said Miss Hopkins carefully.

"I see" said Brandy. "Well, I don't want to keep you chatting here in the hall. Perhaps I will see you again before dinner?" said Brandy, for Denny was tugging at her sleeve.

"Oh . . . but . . . where are you two going?"

"The kitchens!" declared Denny gleefully as he pulled Brandy along.

At their back Deana Hopkins stood frowning. This development was not what she had expected, not what she wanted, and it certainly would not

37

aid her schemes. Indeed, there was every good chance that Brandice Fernwood might get very much in the way. However, she was met with yet another surprise as the library doors opened and two strange men, accompanied by her cousin, Alistair Hayward, emerged. They were bantering merrily until they discovered her presence, where-upon they pulled up and demanded eagerly to be introduced.

A tinker's daughter, a dark-haired, dark-eyed gypsy, a pretty, a maid, a delightful creature who gave joy to her family and would soon marry within the tribe and produce more of her kind. Rose wandered through the sylvan setting swinging her basket of wild watercress. She had come to the stream that ran through Quendon lands, for it was the closest place she knew of to obtain the baby watercress which she meant to use in to-night's dinner. Tonight's dinner . . . a very special occasion for her and her bethrothed.

Suddenly the path she walked was shadowed by the forms of two large men, each carrying an old-fashioned flintlock. *Poachers!* They were illegally hunting on Quendon land. They would say nothing about the watercress, about her presence here; after all, they did not belong here either. So thought the maid after her initial bolt of fear, and then she saw their expressions. Without a word exchanged she started to run. And they were quick to follow.

Denny picked up a broken branch and threw it

high and far. He felt good for the first time in days. He looked worshipfully at Brandy. "I never knew toast and jam could taste so delicious."

She smiled. "Now if only you will hold it. The soda water, sipped slowly, as you did, should help, Denny . . . but I won't make any promises." She sighed. "I should like the doctor to come in and have another look at you."

"No. He will only bleed me . . . and say I am suffering a decline. That's what he does, what he says."

They picked their way through the wooded path, and Brandy glanced behind her. The Abbey was no longer visible. They had been out walking some fifteen minutes. She didn't want to overtax him. "Denny . . . would you like to take me back now or do you mean to walk my legs off?"

"Never say you are tired? Posh!" he exclaimed playfully. He was pleased enough to return, for he was beginning to feel the fatigue play havoc with his limbs.

"I'll have you know that I traveled a goodly distance this day to come to Quendon Abbey and am fully entitled to a rest! Home . . . take me home," she was teasing, reaching out to tickle him, when a girl's short, terrified cry made her spin around.

"Eh, Lade . . . she be the very one whot was dancing at the circus last week," said the larger of the two men as he caught Rose and spun her around.

Rose squirmed in the brute's hold; she kicked

39

and she clawed. She had been warned against such as they. The creature known as Lade scratched his chin and gave it as his opinion that she had indeed been the dancer, though she no longer wore the large hooped earrings she had worn then. He reached out and took her face in his hands.

"Ye be pretty enough wench. What would ye say to pleasing me with a kiss?"

From behind them came Brandice Fernwood. She sized up the situation in an instant and played her part well as she demanded in cold, imperious terms, "Release the child at once!"

Both men spun around, saw that a duchess of a maid was addressing them. Saw young Quendon coming up behind her and knew well they could be in a great deal of trouble.

"We meant no 'arm, miss . . . 'aving a bit a sport, that's all," explained Lade.

"Were you?" She saw them for poachers at once and played her cards well, for she knew that she was unarmed and only boldness would work here. "On Quendon land? I should suggest to you that you make your escape as quickly as possible, as my cousin will soon be along and I don't think he would appreciate either your presence here or your behavior to this young woman!"

"Aye!" agreed both creatures at once and made a hurried departure.

Rose put up her chin. There were scratches on her bare arms where the brambles had ripped at her. Her shawl was on the ground. She bent to pick it up, but Brandy was before her. Their eyes met in friendship as Brandy handed her the shawl midway up from unbending.

"Thank you," said Rose softly.

"Will you return to Quendon Abbey with us? I should like to attend to your bruises . . . and offer you up a cup of tea," asked Brandy kindly.

"No . . . I will be missed at home."

"I shall have you sent home in the carriage," said Denny, at once the young gentleman. "You have been hurt on Quendon land; you must allow me to make it up to you."

Rose felt much in spirits again, and she smiled. "Thank you, young lord, but I must return home."

"Then at leat allow us to escort you—"

"No . . . my camp is not very far. . . ."

"Please," said Denny, "I like listening to you talk . . . you have such a pretty accent . . . and you could tell me all about the gypsies. I have always wanted to be one."

She gave the boy a hug, "You are very dear, young lord, but I shall make better time on my own. If only . . ."

"If only what?" prodded Brandy.

"My basket . . . I must have dropped it." She was hesitant because the basket contained the watercress from Quendon property.

Denny saw it at once, ran, scooped it up and brought it back.

"Here it is."

"Thank you," she said shyly.

Denny had seen the watercress within the folds of the large plaid handkerchief. "You may come

41

and collect watercress on my land anytime you need to."

She thanked them again, and after she was out of sight Denny turned and gave Brandy a sudden joyful hug. In some surprise Brandy returned his caress and patted him on the head.

"Now, my sweet buck, what is all this?"

"You've come and everything will be right and tight now, I just know it. Why . . . we have already started having marvelous adventures!"

FOUR

Hurriedly and with her cloak wrapped tightly around her, Brandy put the house behind her and made for the stables. The morning air was crisp, delicious with its coolness and full with its sunlight. The sky was clear, the air was fragrant with autumn, and Brandy wanted to ride wildly across the fields before she was discovered and inevitably confined.

She reached the stone building that housed the horses, and there a sleepy groom came toward her rubbing his eyes.

"Aye, miss . . . would ye be wanting yer mare?"

"If you will bring my saddle down, I'll tack her myself, thank you," said Brandy agreeably.

His eyes widened, but then any maid who dressed in breeches was quite capable of anything, he silently decided, and went to do her bidding.

She took down her bridle from its wood hanging block, scooped up a curry and brush, and went to her mare, cooing softly to the mare's welcoming snorts.

"Well, Brown Sugar . . . have you missed me?" She slipped a carrot into the mare's nibbling mouth and started the necessary job of currying the horse's coat. The bay mare was already clean, but Brandy enjoyed handling her horse. Quickly she went over her with the dandy brush, picked out the four hooves and brought the Pelham bridle to Brown Sugar's head. The double reins were slipped over the acquiescent animal's head, and a moment later the bit was in and Brandy turned to find the groom holding the saddle for her.

"Would ye be wishful to 'ave me ride behind ye, miss?" His mistress, Miss Lara, never went out alone, but then Miss Lara never wore breeches.

"Thank you, no." Brandy was already leading her mare outdoors, slipping her booted foot into the stirrup, and swinging herself into the saddle.

Brown Sugar was ready for a run, but Brandy kept her in check, insisting that they walk sedately down the drive, trot collectedly onto the riding path, maintaining their checked speed while the mare's ears moved continuously, very much on the alert. This was new country, and the mare was nervous as well as anxious to spend some of her energy.

Brandy laughed, perfectly at ease and fully in control.

"Wait, love . . . I'll let you have your head . . . just wait . . . we'll pick our spot." They rounded

44

the bend in the woods, and it opened onto a great sweeping field of high grass. Brandy eased up on the reins. "Now, love . . ." And they were off across the field.

There is a risk in the speed, there is a thrill in the risk and an exhilaration in the fact that for those moments one can join with the animal and feel. Brandy gave herself over to the joy of running with Brown Sugar and forgot all else . . . and it was good.

Farmer Burley needed new machinery and felt certain Lord Marden would agree to supply him with his requirements. After all, he was his lordship's best-paying tenant, and he had proved himself and his expenditures many times in the past. Even so, he was surprised and a little bit touched when Lord Marden himself and not his lordship's agent came to call and conclude the arrangements.

Happy enough over the unexpected visit, he took his lordship on a tour of the southwest fields. His cob plodded along behind him as he made easy conversation with his landlord. He saw the copper-haired schoolgirl racing across the field. What else could she be, dressed in breeches and a wool cap? It reminded him of the water supply on Quendon land. Only a fence separated him from a piece of Quendon land that the late lord had never seen fit to use or to sell to Marden.

"Would the new young lord be selling that piece, do ye know, m'lord?"

Brandy's glistening red hair was unmistakable,

even at such a distance, or so it was to Lord Marden, who had ever an eye for a beautiful woman. He recognized her at once, took up his reins, and nimbly mounted his dapple gray, turning to the astonished farmer.

"We'll have to see about that, my man. . . . I have to rush, as I just recalled an errand that needed attending to." With this he was off like a shot and taking his fence flying.

Brandy turned to his call and reined her horse in to await his descent. An admiring gleam brightened her green eyes as she appraised his steed, and the compliment rose to her lips easily.

"Prime, my lord! What does he stand . . . sixteen?"

"Sixteen-two, and thank you. I am rather proud of old Cloud here. We've come a long way together." If he was surprised over Brandy's attire, he hid it well.

"Oh . . . did you train him yourself?"

He grinned sheepishly. "I like to think so, but sometimes I wonder if it wasn't he who did the training. But tell me, Miss Fernwood, what brings you out so early this morning?"

She laughed, and he was tickled by the sound. "My mode of dress, sir."

"Eh?" He knew full well what she meant, but he wanted to hear her go on about it.

"Well, I couldn't very well ride about the countryside clothed as I am now during the . . . er . . . fashionable hours, now could I?"

"I don't see why not. I think you look charming." His smile twinkled in his aqua-blue eyes.

46

"Ah, but then I am persuaded that you are one of a kind, my lord."

"As you are, Miss Fernwood . . . so answer another question if you will?"

"Perhaps."

"Just what are you doing in the Cotswolds when London must be in full swing at this moment?"

"My lord," she said, smiling wide, "I have had three seasons of London in full swing. I do assure you that I am missing little."

"Three seasons? Impossible." He was genuinely incredulous.

"Why impossible?"

"How have you managed to remain unattached?"

"I have managed it very well, thank you," she answered, twinkling up at him, for this seemed to be a recurring question more and more these days than ever before.

He was thoughtful a moment, and then a gleam lit his eyes. "Aha. So that answers my question regarding Fisk's presence here. No doubt he is one of your suitors."

She said nothing to this but took hold of the conversation by directing him an arched look that nearly took his breath away. "And, my lord . . . what of you? I find it hard to believe that an out-and-outer, a nonesuch, a veritable whip, a corinthian of your social standing—for Fisk has assured me you are all these things—that I have not had you pointed out to me during one of my seasons!"

Dryly he said, "In spite of what you have been led to believe, the sad truth, my beauty, is that I have something of a . . . er . . . *reputation*. It is not

47

surprising that you would not have had me pointed out to you. In fact, I rather think your cousin, Sir Reggie, was at pains to shield you from me and my kind."

It was obvious what he meant. He was even admitting to it. All she could say to this was a long-drawn-out "Oh."

"And though your name comes to mind—for, my girl, you are hailed at White's Club as the 'Incomparable'—I have not before seen you or I assure you I would have sought you out." He sighed. "Sad it is to say, I twiddled away your first season in Greece with Hobhouse and Byron, your second I was in Scotland with my married sister and her numerous offspring . . . but your third season I was certainly in London, sporadically but enough to have heard your name mentioned." He smiled widely at her. "They did not lie."

She ignored this last and urged her horse into a canter. He was far too self-assured, and Reggie or no, she had had her share of rakes. They were all engaging and quite without principles. He seemed very much like most of his kind, and she must not allow herself to be won over by a pretty remark and a winning smile!

They reached the woods lining the great stone wall. Beyond loomed the Abbey and its ruins. They schooled their horses down to a sedate pace as they weaved their way through the trees and etched out a path.

Marden inclined his handsome head. "Beyond that wall is the finest garden in all of the Cotswolds. Denny Quendon's great-grandfather had a maze

48

of Spanish design installed. I wish you could see it in the spring and summer when it is in full bloom."

She eyed him speculatively. All trace of his earlier tone was gone. He seemed no longer bent on flirting with her. He had understood the look in her eye and he had backed away from his purpose. Excellent. She liked that.

"Tell me, my lord ... are there no ghosts at Quendon?"

"Of course ... but only one that I know of," he anwered at once.

"Oh, how wonderful. Who is he? What does he want?" she demanded gleefully.

"It is said that during the Reformation a young and lovely maid came upon the Abbey during the time it housed a group of priests. One of the priests was a young man and he promptly fell in love with her. The story goes that a brash nobleman was in pursuit of the girl and traced her to Quendon Abbey, where he discovered her and made to take her. The priest, without thinking, jumped in to defend her, but as he had never used a sword before, the nobleman cut him down. His name was Dominique, and he is often heard on stormy nights calling for his love."

"Oh, how perfectly horrible. The poor man ... the poor girl ..."

He grinned. "We can turn in here. It will lead us to the courtyard."

A few moments later, having left their horses with the grooms at the stable, they were entering the house bantering and laughing over the likelihood of the ghost story. Their laughter was easy and bright, and it brought Denny scurrying down the back hall.

"Marden . . . Brandy . . . the very two people I want to see!" announced the young man.

"Aha! That warrants no good, Miss Fernwood, depend upon it."

"Unjust," cried the youth. "Only wait until you hear."

"You look very well, Denny."

"Hmmm. I do, don't I? I ate that toast . . . and the hothouse peach you gave me. I drank down the soda water, though I think I would have preferred some nice lemonade. But since I did what you wanted, Brandy . . . you couldn't say no to me, could you?"

"Say no to you?" she returned warily. "About what, Denny?"

"Why, the circus!"

Brandy and Marden exchanged glances, and Marden said, "Why don't we retire to the library, where Miss Fernwood may be comfortable with a cup of tea"—he held up a hand—"and then you may plague her all you like."

She turned on Marden in something of a huff. "Very fine speaking, my lord, for the thing is he *will* plague me, and well you know it!"

They reached the library, where the fire was ablaze. Marden stood back to watch Brandy drop off her cloak and wool cap and run a hand over her long copper curls. She was magnificent. All of a sudden she seemed conscious of her clothes. Doubtfully she glanced at Marden. "I should go up and change before Cynthia Hayward comes down."

"She won't be down for hours," stuck in Denny impatiently. "She don't like to move about before noon. Now, Brandy, do say yes . . . for Lara won't go and I should like to go to the circus."

"Where is this circus?" Marden asked on a laugh, for he could see that Brandy was at a momentary loss.

"That's what is so famous. 'Tis but a gypsy camp giving it . . . and I've never even seen a gypsy carnival, except once when Papa took me to London. . . But, oh, Marden, do say you will take us. Brandy would love it so."

"Would you, Miss Fernwood?" he quizzed her.

"Of course she would. She wears breeches, don't she? That ought to tell you what a right 'un she is. Do say yes, Marden, for I do see she couldn't very well take me on her own." He lowered his voice. "She is, you know, a girl."

"I . . . er . . . can see that," said Marden. "Well then, Miss Fernwood, he does seem rather in spirits . . . much like his old self. What say you?"

Brandy studied Denny's face. He was still pale and there was still a dryness about his skin that worried her, but he did seem full of vigor, and this was a good sign. No depression here.

"When do we go?"

He jumped and clapped his hands together. "Famous! Tonight . . . before dinner, though, just as it gets dark. And we shall have to learn the way of it from Jeffreys. Jeffreys will know."

*   *   *

51

The night holds a certain magic for children and adults alike, but for the child it holds one thing more—the forbidden. It is a space of darkness, of mysterious delights, of dancing, of music, of late-hour feasts, and it is withheld from the child. There too is the aura of goblins, elves on the prowl, and intrigue only awaiting to be discovered.

Denny sat huddled between Lord Marden and Brandy in the open-perch phaeton, and his eyes were open wide with expectation. Brandy observed this and smiled to herself before stealing the briefest glance at his lordship. His profile was magnetically masculine, ruggedly handsome, sensuously pleasing, and silently she whipped herself for her lapse. Careful, girl! The hour was not yet past eight, but the night was quite progressed, such were the stars, such was the moon, and in spite of herself Brandy felt a rush of tingling anticipation.

Beside them rode Fisk on horseback, babbling in his fashion to Marden, who kept up an easy stream of conversation. They led another coach, Sir Reginald's, which contained Lara, Deana Hopkins, and Alistair Hayward. The announcement that Marden and Brandy were taking young Quendon to the carnival was all that was needed for an expedition to start up.

Brandy's green eyes again appraised Marden. His actions tonight did not fit with the unfavorable impression she had of his character. He had come in his phaeton to collect Denny, apologizing to her for the inconvenience.

"You see," he explained, "I thought it would be a treat for Denny."

"A treat?" cried Lara. "I only hope he does not come down with a cold!"

Brandy's green eyes chided Lara. She would have to speak to her friend later and find out what it was she held against Lord Marden, for there was certainly something there. "Don't worry, Lara," she said gently. "It is such a warm evening, and Denny will have his cloak to wrap around himself as well as a blanket if need be."

"That's right," agreed Denny. "You mustn't coddle me, Lara. I'm not a baby, you know." He sighed over the problem, for his sister still did not seem satisfied. "And besides . . . Brandy will be with me to help keep me warm, so you see, there can be no objection."

Brandy's eyes widened for upon seeing the open phaeton she had quite made up her mind to go in the coach with Sir Reginald. Whether this had to do with fear of discomfort or fear of being alone with Marden she had not yet thought about. Marden at this leaned over and said for Brandy's ears alone, "He is quite right, you know, Miss Fernwood. Denny will be all warm and toasty wedged between us." He had a devilish look in his aqua eyes.

She was not overset by his audaciousness. She gave him an arched look and said, equally as quietly, "Oh, yes, as long as we keep him *between* us, my lord."

Thus the party began its excursion, and now

53

she could hear the carnival not far ahead. "I hear it! I hear it!" squealed Denny joyfully.

Indeed the trees seemed to shake with the resonance of riotous laughter and merrymaking. Music, ribald, undignified, and totally inviting, filtered through as well. Torches blazed and could be seen as the party made the bend in the road. They were most definitely approaching the carnival.

Dark-haired, dark-eyed gypsy boys came scurrying up to take charge of the horses and carriages, promising to do all that was necessary while their owners enjoyed themselves at the gypsy camp.

Marden came around to take Brandy into his hands. Denny jumped nimbly off, anxious to hurry into the circle of carnival-goers. Marden's strong grip held Brandy's waist as he lowered her to the ground and held her close. He had a sudden almost uncontrollable urge to bend, to find her lips . . . but no, what was he, some young fool?

Gypsy maids in flamboyant colors passed with baskets on their hips calling, "Fresh buns, ho . . ."

There were stands between the tents, and the aroma of hot apple cider was entrancing. There were jugglers and performing dogs, and finally with a yelp of pure delight Denny was off to get a closer view of the performing bear.

Fisk brought their attention to a gaily decorated dais where a gray-haired man with a black top hat and black cape was holding up his black wand for attention. He had a crowd gathered, and a young boy was going among them collecting payment in advance for the show they were about to enjoy.

"I say . . . a magic show! Are you coming?"

"Perhaps later, Fisk . . . I think Miss Fernwood would enjoy a tour of the camp first," said Marden with a smile of dismissal.

Fisk might have objected had not the lure of the magician been so strong. He had a penchant for such entertainment and reasoned that Brandy would be safe enough with Marden in such a crowd. After all, the devil couldn't seduce her here, with the whole world looking on.

Brandy's green eyes were as wide as Denny's. She had never been at a gypsy carnival. Everything was so vibrant, so alive, so boisterous and wondrously inviting. There too was the security of his lordship beside her. She had only to look towards the man selling the apple cider to find a cup in her hand. Marden was totally attuned to her desires, so deft at attaining whatever she wished. He managed to move her through the crowd of people without allowing a one to touch her, brush by her. She was strangely aware of all this as they toured the grounds.

He was all too conscious of her. She was a woman, a minx, and her open pleasure at everything she saw was captivating. He could not remember ever enjoying himself more, ever being so totally absorbed with another being. Everything about her caught his interest, intrigued him to penetrate further. Her hood had fallen away from her head and her copper tresses were in wild profusion around her face. She was a beauty.

More and more he was hit by this fact. He would have to be careful if he was to stick by his rules. He did not tamper with virgins.

Denny came charging towards them and took up a hand from each of them. "Come on!" he demanded.

"Where to?" Marden laughed.

"To see Daniel Lambert. They say he weighs *fifty-three stones*. Come on!"

"Impossible. No one could weigh fifty-three stones," cried Brandy as she felt herself tugged along.

However, Lord Marden paid the admittance fee of three pennies, and acquired the best seats under the tent, and there they discovered that Daniel Lambert was as wide as he was tall, and that was in itself an accomplishment, as he was five feet eleven inches. They were shown the wagon that had been built specially for him and invited to dine at his inn in Leicester.

Deana smiled sweetly at Alistair Hayward, and he was reminded of a kitten purring. His hand reached out and cupped her chin.

"Oh, Deana . . . don't look at me like that."

"Why, Alistair . . . don't you want me?"

His voice went suddenly intense and he took up her shoulders and pressed her against the back of the gypsy wagon. There was no one about and only woods at their back. "Want you?" he growled. "Devil is that I do and you know it!" His mouth taught her some of this, and then he pulled away as though in agony.

She reached and caught his hand and held him at her side.

"Alistair . . ."

"What good is it?" His voice was hoarse. "I have nothing to offer you."

"So . . . you would marry Lara. Is that the way to a fortune?"

"Perhaps," he said softly, ignoring the look that came into her eyes.

"She won't make you happy!" snapped Deana. "Only I know how to do that. Alistair . . . look at me. . . ."

He did, and it drew a sigh from his inner being. Did he love her? She certainly made him feel. She was so lovely. The moonlight glistened on her dark hair. She was young and full of promise, and something more. . . . He took her hand, kissed it softly.

"This is no good, Deana. It will end in heartache for us both. Come . . . they will be wondering where we are."

No one was in fact wondering where Deana and Alistair were. This very naturally was due to the fact that each member of their group was finding total rapture in pursuits never before undertaken. Denny, satisfied that both Marden and Brandy were properly impressed with Daniel Lambert, proceeded to lead them to Ramus, the performing bear. There he attempted to win a stick away from Ramus. This proved difficult in the extreme, as Ramus seemed particularly fond of the stick. There was no telling how long the two would have competed for the stick had not Fisk descended upon them.

"Devilish good, that magician . . ." His eyes told him that a bear was sniffing his legs, and he began backing away. "I say!" He was not about to show any fear with Brandy watching. "A bear, you know."

"Yes," agreed Denny. "Isn't he famous!"

Fisk was spared the necessity of a reply as a musical fanfare called for quiet, whereupon it was announced that a special treat was in store for them at the cost of only two pennies per person. Rose, the gypsy princess, was about to dance.

Brandy looked up and saw the dark-haired girl she had helped in the woods the other day. The girl was heavily made up with eye blacking and rouge, but recognizable all the same. She smiled at her as Rose passed by, but the gypsy girl continued on her way.

Sir Reginald took Lara's hand and stopped her. Everyone seemed to be moving towards the gypsy dancing tent, but he had to talk to her. "I . . . I missed you, Lara . . . far more than I can tell you now." He watched her intensely, waited hopefully.

She blushed and kept her gaze averted. Her heart trembled, and her fingers were not quite steady. She had hurt him, she could see that, but if she had accepted to be his wife, she would have hurt him so much more. If she had accepted his proposal of marriage she would have had to tell him the truth about her mother. She could not do that. That was impossible, for Denny must never know! He saw her recede into her shell and frowned. His hands clenched themselves at his back. He had to keep himself in check.

"Why, Lara? I deserve an explanation. You left without giving me one ... but now I am asking, why?"

"Why?" She looked straight ahead. "I don't understand."

He was exasperated by her response. Why did she play games? She wasn't like that. "Lara ... must I beg for crumbs? Very well then, throw some my way. Look at me, explain to me what happened. Explain why you allowed me to ... come so near and then denied me. Lara, why would you not have me?"

She did look at him then, and she was near to tears. "My father's death changed everything. You don't understand, and I am not ... not able to tell you more. Indeed, I did not realize ... had nearly forgotten my responsibilities. I should not have encouraged you this summer. It was wrong of me."

"Then you admit it. You cared ... you *did* encourage me to think I had some hope?"

"Please, Reginald ... do not press me further," she begged.

He restrained himself. Perhaps Brandy would help him to discover what it was that Lara was afraid of. His hope had been renewed. It was not because she did not love him. Indeed, there was every indication that she did. He led her quietly towards their party, who were now watching Rose dance among them.

FIVE

The morning was damp. Dark clouds hovered and a wind was whipping at the trees. It was strange weather for a ride across the fields, but Brandy, her hair blowing in the swirling gusts, was doing just that.

Something had gone wrong. Denny had taken a sudden turn for the worse, and it made no sense. He had eaten sensibly at dinner. He had eaten only fruit and sweet buns at the carnival, and Brandy had been pleased with the renewed color in his cheeks.

This morning Denny was deathly pale, he was dazed, not quite coherent, and his nose had bled for no earthly reason. Why? What had happened during the night? He hadn't eaten after they arrived home. Of course there was the milk, the warm milk that Lara herself had taken up to him, just to settle him after his exciting evening.

She couldn't forget the way Lara and her aunt had exchanged glances when she said the doctor must be sent for. What was wrong with them? What was it Lara was afraid of? Why did her aunt have such control over her?

The damp went through her clothes and chilled her muscles, but she had to ride and think this out, because there was an answer. It was there ready, waiting to be said out loud, but she dared not even think it!

What other answer was there? Over and over again it presented itself to her. Ghastly it was to suggest, even to herself, yet possible, so very possible.

The nosebleed had brought it all rushing back to mind. Her friend Caroline came vividly into the picture. Caroline, poor Caroline, who had died so many years ago. Caroline, who had slowly, unwittingly, poisoned herself with *arsenic*.

Caroline was not a beauty, so she had compensated with face creams, finally mixing a drop of arsenic with her lotions. She progressed from there to taking a mixture of it orally, and then she had begun to act strangely. She often seemed confused, dazed, listless. Her complexion turned deathly pale, and all this without anyone knowing why.

No one understood because at that time Caroline kept it a well-guarded secret. No one knew about the arsenic. Then she began having the nosebleeds and the fainting spells. Just when she could keep a doctor away no longer she went into one last faint. *Arsenic, arsenic, arsenic!*

61

What could she do? Brandy was frightened, really frightened, because if Denny was suffering the same symptoms it meant, really meant, that someone was giving him arsenic, that he was being poisoned! Why? Why poison a little boy? Because he was Lord Quendon and as such was a titled, wealthy little man. Who stood to gain by his death? My God . . . Lara? No, not Lara . . . it couldn't be Lara!

She slowed her mare to a trot and wielded her easily through the tangle of trees to the private drive that led to the Marden Estates. Before her the great Tudor-styled home loomed in mellow beauty. She would go to Marden. It was absurd . . . but Marden cared about Denny and she wanted to hear what Marden had to say about Denny's sudden turn for the worse.

Denny. Poor Denny. Would the doctor realize? He had to realize. The doctors had said they could have helped if Caroline had come to them. She hadn't, though. She had been too afraid her mother would discover what she had done . . . she was too afraid of scandal. *Scandal?* The school had rocked with it after Caroline's death. There had been total chaos.

She dismounted near the large, neat stables, where a young stableboy came up to her and took the reins of her horse.

"She needs to be walked down."

"Aye, that she does, miss. . . . Lord but she be in somethin' of a sweat."

Brandy pressed a coin into the boy's hand, and he took it willingly. If he was surprised by her mode of dress, he kept it to himself. There was no saying what the quality would do next.

The large dark oak door was opened wide by a tall, thin butler who looked Brandy over once. His experience told him that although she wore breeches beneath her velvet cloak, there was most certainly the air of the blood here.

"May I see his lordship, please?" inquired Brandy. "You may tell him Miss Fernwood to see him . . . and 'tis urgent."

Lord Marden was closeted with his man of business in his book-lined study. He saw a familiar form skip up his stone steps to his front door and he was up in an instant.

"Balden . . . excuse me . . ."

"But my lord . . . the books."

"Do them as best you can without me." His expression was stern.

Balden had been serving his lordship nearly three years now and was quick to understand that Marden's mood had suddenly turned grim. He had no idea why, but he knew better than to argue with him.

"Miss Fernwood . . . what a pleasant surprise. But not my dear, a very wise one." There was a look of disapproval on his face.

She knew, of course, that he was right. His was a bachelor's residence. There was no female in his home to act as hostess and spare her reputation. She was breaking society's rules. However, she had no time to waste on rules.

"Please, my lord . . . can you return to Quendon Abbey with me? I will explain along the way."

63

He took but a moment to search her eyes, and what he found made him act swiftly.

"My coat and hat, please, and do tell Balden I may be gone for the rest of the morning."

The butler disappeared only a moment and returned with the required items, helping his lordship into his riding coat before standing back to watch Marden take up Brandy's arm and lead her outdoors.

He waited only till they were mounted and on their way before turning and demanding firmly but yet gently, "If you will be so kind Miss Fernwood . . . what is this all about?"

"Denny. He . . . he has taken a sad turn, my lord." She was much agitated.

"That is impossible. He was better last night . . . I am sure of it."

"You are quite right. He was better, though Cynthia Hayward would have it that his excursion last night has done him in. 'Tis not so, my lord. That is not what he is suffering from."

"Nooo," said his lordship slowly, "I do not think his frolic at the carnival last night did him any harm . . . but that will be for the doctor to confirm."

"Are you . . . are you angry that I have drawn you into this?" She felt ridiculously shy all at once.

"Nonsense. I am honored that you thought to advise me of this. Denny is very dear to me." He studied her face a long moment as they trotted through the woods, taking the shortcut to the

Abbey drive. "Brandy . . . Miss Fernwood . . . there is more you are not telling me."

"What can you mean?"

"There is something troubling you . . . and you seemed reluctant to mention it. You came to fetch me . . . therefore you must wish to trust me. Why don't you take a chance? Do trust me."

Every instinct told her to confide in him, but she couldn't. He might think her a fool, and after all, she could be wrong. The doctor would soon be with Denny and they would know. She must keep it to herself for now.

She shook her head. " 'Tis nothing. Look, there is the doctor's carriage on the drive. He must already be with Denny."

They were at the double brass-studded doors a few moments later, and Brandy was rushing past Jeffreys, ignoring his flicker of amazement as he noticed her style of dress. She turned round to put a hand to Lord Marden.

"I must hurry if I am to change before Cynthia Hayward finds me out. She does not approve. . . . But do go into the library. I shan't be long."

Fire and damnation, he cursed softly to himself as he did her bidding. Here he was being ordered about by a slip of a girl. It was intolerable. She was a problem he would soon have to deal with. Perhaps he would leave for London sooner than he had planned. He moved to the library, found Jeffreys opening the door before him, and was met by a cozy scene within.

Lara stood by the fireplace, her lovely face

drawn in sadness, in worry, in doubt. Sir Reginald stood within touching distance, his hands clasped behind his back, his eyes soothing, looking for her own.

Fisk paced to and fro near the doors that led to the conservatory. Alistair Hayward sat behind the gothic desk; his quill worked furiously across a ledger sheet, but his eyes darted towards the doors just as Marden entered.

Only Fisk rushed across the room to welcome thankfully this new arrival on the scene.

"By Jove, Marden, devilishly glad you are here. There is coffee, you know." Then in aside, "You would do much better with a glass of sherry . . . considering . . . had two glasses m'self you know."

"Lord Marden . . . what are you doing here?" asked Lara quietly.

"Miss Fernwood was kind enough to advise me of Denny's state of health this morning. I came because I am interested, Miss Quendon, in knowing the results of the doctor's efforts."

"No doubt he has a chill after last night," fretted Lara.

Sir Reginald took the fist she put to her mouth and held it in both hands. "No, Lara . . . you mustn't despair." His voice was soft, soothing. She glanced worshipfully at him.

Alistair Hayward ran a hand through his light-brown locks and stood up. "No . . . we must not despair, nor must we hold out false hopes. We must face the situation and be brave." He was moving towards Lara.

The door opened again and Deana, her dark

66

short hair waved glisteningly around her attractive face, scanned the assembled group. Quietly she entered the room. Hayward turned from his purpose and smiled warmly, welcomingly, at her. She looked lovely in the simple gown of pale-blue cambric.

"Deana . . . I am so glad you have come," said Hayward. "You will know just how to cheer Lara into better spirits."

"Stop it! stop it!" cried Lara, suddenly overcome. "I don't need any cheering. It is Denny . . . my poor Denny . . ."

Fisk bent towards Marden. "You see, man? Sticky business, this. Brandy didn't tell me things would go like this."

"Had you known, you cawker, you still would have followed her here."

Fisk sighed. "That's a truth."

Marden grinned at him. "But you are out, you know."

"Eh . . . what the devil do you mean?"

"She won't have you in the end," said Marden quietly.

Fisk thought of retorting, thought of Brandy, and sighed.

"That's another truth . . . but the thing is that I've known her any number of years now. Reggie's cousin, you know . . . was wont to meet her at his mother's all the time . . . crept up on me that she would make an excellent Mrs. Fisk. I think she is in my blood, Marden."

Marden smiled. "You would be better off purged, my friend."

Dr. Henry Franklin wiped the perspiration off his brow, knocked gently on Cynthia Hayward's sitting-room door, waited for her response, and entered the pink-and-silver room. Nothing about its decor had been changed since Lady Quendon had used the room, and as it suited the present occupant well enough, Mrs. Hayward declined to bother Lara about redecorating it.

Franklin was a large man whose clothes of country wools fit him loosely and comfortably. He had a shock of steely gray hair, wide gray brows over pale-gray eyes. His nose was hawked, his chin round, and the lips were full and sensuous. Until recently Cynthia had found him amusing, desirable and pleasant enough company. Until recently.

Franklin found everything about Cynthia Hayward captivating. He was a widower. He was childless. He was lonely. She was lovely, she was clever, entertaining, warm-blooded, bewitching, and interested in him. However, things were going awry, and he was caught up in what was turning out to be a web of trouble.

"Cynthia . . ." He went towards her. She met him, her ivory silks rustling about her full-bodied figure. "I have missed you more than I can say. I . . . I am ill with apprehension over this . . . nasty business."

She turned away from him. "Would you like some hot tea, Henry?"

"No, my love." He pursued her, took her shoulders, turned her to face him. "We must talk, Cynthia."

"Talk? Why, of course, Henry. What would you like to talk about?"

He appraised her from head to toe. Her dark shining ringlets were piled high on her well-shaped head. Her lips were full, ripe . . . he wanted her, but things were moving dangerously out of his control. He steeled himself.

"You know full well what I need to talk about, Cynthia, what we both must face. A decision must be made."

"I dislike making decisions. Hayward always made them for me when he was alive . . . and now my son makes them."

He rather thought this was true. Cynthia was a dominant force. He doubted that she ever allowed her fate to be ruled by another. "Cynthia . . . it has passed the line . . . whatever happens from here on in . . . involves me."

"I don't know what you are talking about. How is young Denny?"

"Denny is ill. Dangerously ill. Near death, Cynthia . . . and *I* will be asked why!"

"Why? Don't you know why?"

"I am very nearly certain that I do know why," he shouted.

"Nearly certain. Well, you cannot go shocking the family without telling them it is a certainty, now can you, Henry?"

"Cynthia, if he dies, I shall have to sign the death certificate."

"So you will, my love."

He took her in his arms roughly. "Do you think I could hurt you . . . hurt someone who is dear to you?"

"I trust you implicitly, my love."

"God help me. . . ." He thought on what he was, on what he had been, and Henry Franklin was near, very near to weeping.

Brandy rushed to her chamber, splashed herself with warm water from her basin, threw off her clothes as her maid clucked and chided, and quickly slid into a cream-colored velvet whose lace dipped low over the open heart-shaped bodice which traveled to the waist, where it was met by a wide brown velvet band. From there the velvet fell in a straight line to Brandy's well-formed ankles. Cream velvet slippers covered her stockinged feet. A locket went around the neck, and hurriedly Francy brushed Brandy's copper curls into a semblance of order, tied it with a brown velvet band at the top of her head, caught the tips of hair and curled them with her finger, and then pinned them to Brandy's head. She looked a picture indeed as she scurried down the hall and stopped short to watch Dr. Franklin enter Mrs. Hayward's sitting-room door.

It occurred to her that she might attempt to eavesdrop. She chided herself and resolutely went past, took the stairs, went down the main hall, reached the doorknob, found that Jeffreys had attained it before her, laughed over the matter, and entered the gloomy room.

SIX

This would do not one iota of good, thought Brandy as she surveyed the dismal faces of the assembled company in the library. Look at Lara, far too pale; at this rate she would be falling ill. She needed to be cheered up. She put up her chin and took all attention with her musical if rather admonishing reproach.

"What poor-spirited creatures we have here! What is this?"

Lara turned toward her friend, and her blue eyes were filled with worry. "Brandy . . . oh, Brandy . . ."

"Stop it this instant! What is this? Self-pity? What will Denny think if he hears of this gloom? Do you want him afraid for himself?"

"No . . . no, of course not. You are right," faltered Lara.

Brandy patted her shoulder. "Now tell me, Lara m'girl . . . why hasn't the doctor come to you with his report? You are Denny's sister, and it is to you he should come after his examination of Denny."

"What do you mean? Never say he has left already."

"No. But—"

The door of the library opened once again, and this time Cynthia Hayward glided within, her face a masque of misery. She stopped at the sight of Lara and clenched her hands together at her waist as though in agony.

"Lara . . . dearest . . . I fear we . . . I must talk with you."

It was more than Lara could bear. Her hopes went flying. Here was her aunt pronouncing Denny's death. It was written all over Cynthia's face, and Lara could not stand the strain. She gasped, her knees wobbled, her legs gave way, and she sank lightly to the oriental carpet in a faint.

Brandy was on the floor beside her at once. She chafed Lara's hands together and looked up to find that Lord Marden was taking command.

"Smelling salts!" he demanded of Mrs. Hayward. He had kept silent, in the background. He had maintained the position of interested observer as the actors played out their script, but this called for his intervention.

Mrs. Hayward was shaken by Lara's reaction to her words. She had thought she was being particularly gentle. She hurried to the sideboard medicine cabinet and produced the required item. This she put into Marden's outstretched hand. In turn he bent to his knees beside Brandy and gave them to her quietly.

"I think, Miss Fernwood, you will find this helpful."

Brandy thanked him breathlessly and waved the inhalant several times beneath Lara's dainty nose. The girl jerked away from the heady aroma.

"That's the ticket!" cried Fisk, leaning over Brandy to see the outcome.

Lara's eyelashes fluttered and she whispered pathetically, "Denny . . . ?"

Sir Reginald, much moved by all this, found it impossible to speak, but he was there, holding her up by her shoulders, lifting her into a sitting position, while Brandy directed the situation.

"Carry her to the sofa, Reg . . . there . . . that's right." She then turned to Cynthia Hayward and in some irritation demanded, "Mrs. Hayward, perhaps it would be kinder if you just told us what it is the doctor has reported about Denny. It is what we have all been waiting to hear . . . it is what he should have come first to Lara with, as she is the boy's legal guardian!"

Marden watched, and a gleam of admiration came to his eye. The chit was quite beautiful when in a rage, and something of a duchess was in her mien. Incredible. Rarely had he ever seen a maid take such control.

He was not alone in this thought. Mrs. Hayward was much shaken by Brandy's authoritive air. She felt temporarily at a loss.

"I . . . er . . . the doctor and I are good friends,

73

you see . . . he thought I would be . . . better equipped to break the news to my niece."

"Did he? What news is that?" What was this? thought Brandy. Didn't the doctor recognize the fact that Denny was being poisoned? What was happening here? But then that might be the problem. If the doctor saw that Denny was being poisoned, it meant someone in the Quendon household was a killer!

Mrs. Hayward didn't realize that Brandy was giving her, and giving the doctor, the benefit of the doubt. She stumbled right in.

"I don't know that I should be announcing this before a household of guests . . . but though the news is of concern only for the family . . . perhaps it is best that I tell you and—"

"Without speeches, Mrs. Hayward. What did the doctor have to say?" demanded Brandy harshly. She had decided the previous night at dinner that she had no liking for Cynthia Hayward. This opinion was reestablished as she watched the woman's face. There was something evil here.

Cynthia Hayward looked to Lara and said softly, "Our poor Denny . . . suffers from . . ." She trembled to say it. This was the first step she took: ". . . *consumption*."

This was all that was needed to subjugate Lara and reduce her to sobs. Sir Reginald held her close as she wept against his shoulder.

Alistair Hayward thought it was his own shoulder Lara should be using, but instead he found Deana's hand in his own. He pressed it reassuringly and went towards his mother.

"This cannot be true! The boy is so young. . . ."

Deana Hopkins went to her aunt and put an arm about the woman's shoulders. "Poor Aunt Cynthia . . . you have had to bear all this."

Cynthia patted her niece's hand, "Thank you, my dear. At least *you* understand."

Marden and Brandy exchanged glances. This was impossible, said Brandy's eyes. Denny . . . comsumption? Impossible. Her thoughts were instantly understood by Marden, and once again he interjected himself into the scene.

"Perhaps it is time to call in a specialist from London?"

"I don't think that is necessary. Henry Franklin is one of the best doctors in the Cotswolds!" said Cynthia quickly. "Why should the boy be tortured with more doctors poking at him?"

"Because Franklin could be wrong. A second opinion would be a wise course of action," returned Brandy.

"I say," put in Fisk, "I know just the chap. I'm sure he would come up if I dropped him a line. Good sort of fellow, looks after m'sister's spawns. . . ."

"In the meantime . . . perhaps there is something we can do to make Denny more comfortable?" put in Sir Reginald. He had by this time calmed Lara, and he was smiling at her, attempting to bolster her spirits.

Alistair looked doubtfully at his mother. "Is there something in particular we could do for Denny?"

75

It was not his mother but Brandy that answered this question.

"Oh yes," she said distinctly, "there is something that will answer wondrously."

"What is that?" asked Lara hopefully.

"We can *change his diet!*" answered Brandy, watching the Haywards for a reaction. She was not bowled over to find a look of wariness come into Cynthia's eyes. Alistair looked doubtful, which was not surprising, but what did catch her interest was the look of hatred that glinted in Deana Hopkins' brown eyes.

She moved towards Lara and put out her hand, waited for Lara to respond, helped the girl to her feet, and announced to the assembled group, "If you will excuse us, there is something we two must attend to immediately."

Lara's fingers trembled in Brandy's hand, but Brandy silenced the girl with her eyes. It was not until they were hurrying down the corridor to the kitchen that Brandy turned and whispered, "Lara . . . Lara, I am not going to tell you what I think is happening here. I am only going to tell you that for the next few days I am going to take charge of Denny. I want control over his meals. Nothing is to be served to the lad that I have not seen to myself. I want control over the preparation of his food."

"What are you saying? Please, Brandy . . . what is happening?"

"Never mind. I am asking you to *trust me.*"

Long ago when Lara had come to Mrs. Widdons' Select Seminary for young ladies, she had been shy, unpopular, lonely, and very unhappy. Brandy had reached out a hand and said, "Trust me." Lara had been doing just that ever since. She wasn't about to change her habit now!

As Brandy jotted off a letter to her aunt, she carefully avoided all mention of her activities of the last three days. Three days of anxious mothering, pampering, guarding, always guarding— but it had been worth the strain. Lord, but it had been worth it, for Denny was holding down his food, the nosebleeds had stopped, and some of the gray in his face had left him.

It had not been easy, for everyone seemed bent on sneaking up food to Denny! At first Brandy was amazed to find even Alistair had left the boy some chocolates. Thank God Denny had obeyed her. From the outset she had warned him.

"Denny . . . humor me in this. No matter who brings you a treat, whether it is a sweet or just some hot milk, thank them and do not touch it."

"Why?" He was so tired, so tired. He almost didn't care, but there was something in Brandy's eyes that dragged his spirit up.

"Because I have a notion I want to put into effect, and that means you must eat only what I give you. Promise?"

"Yes, Brandy, I promise."

"Not even from Lara, Denny."

"I promise, Brandy."

Thus it was that same evening she allowed him a sip of soda water at fifteen-minute intervals and a bite of toast. He wanted to gulp the soda water down, for he was dehydrated, but she controlled him. He was near to tears, but he maintained his composure and after some two hours his meal of a single piece of toast and a cup of soda water had been consumed.

She left Denny to sleep with Lara beside his bed and went below to find Sir Reginald. She found him alone in the library with a book he was attempting to concentrate on.

"Where is Fisk?"

"Off with Marden. Said the place was too freakish for him and from here on in he was staying at Marden Towers."

"No . . . are you giving me a round tale? Fisk took his things and left?"

"No, said he would send Marden's carriage for his trunks. He only took a portmanteau with an overnight change."

"And you allowed it, Reg?"

"Well, after all . . . we did drag him up here . . . might as well let him amuse himself. He'll be happier at Marden's, you know."

"Yes, I suppose. Anyway, Reg, I want to talk to you."

"Eh?" He looked at her warily. There was a tone in her voice that made him uneasy. Things were certainly bad enough without Brandy's getting too heavily involved.

"Reginald . . . don't look like that. This . . . this is very serious, so I want you to listen carefully to what I am about to tell you."

"Very well."

"When I was up at school . . . and still only

78

fourteen or so . . . a girl, Caroline Stanhope . . . you are well acquainted with her family . . ."

"Yes . . . what has—"

"Shh! She was older than most of us and about to enter the polite world. She was consumed with the desire of making an advantageous marriage and thought that if only she could improve her complexion, which was not good . . . well, never mind.

"Caroline read somewhere about the Gunning Sisters and how they used arsenic in their powders to improve their complexions. It was rumored about the school that Caroline was indulging. . . . No one thought anything of it, though, until she started getting ill.

"She was frightened that her mother would discover what she had been doing, so she hid the fact that she was seriously ill, hid the fact that she was still taking arsenic. She didn't connect the two facts, you see. Suddenly . . . you know what happened. They called it a spasm . . . but everyone knew it was arsenic poisoning."

"Yes, yes, I remember something of the scandal. The poor child. . . . But what has her death to do with us now?"

"One day I was struck by her fingernails. Reggie . . . they had these strange markings. Denny has those markings on his fingernails! Near the end Caroline suffered from nosebleeds—"

"Stop it!" he cut her off sharply. "I see what you are doing and you will stop it at once." He was furious.

"Reg . . . there were times in the classroom

79

when she seemed a veritable dunce. It was because she was fatigued, weak from the poisoning of her system. *She* wasn't suffering from consumption, and Reginald, *neither is Denny!*"

"This is preposterous. What are you saying, Brandy? Think what you are saying!"

"I am saying that Denny is being poisoned," she said gravely.

"By whom?" He got up and paced the room in agitation. "Who stands to gain? Lara? Only think what you are saying!" he repeated, running his hand through his fair hair.

"No, not Lara. . . . Denny must have a male heir. I intend to discover who that heir is."

"I think you are wrong, Brandy, and I forbid you to take this wild suspicion to Lara."

"I have no intention of doing so until I am certain." She tilted her head. "Reg . . . if careful guarding over Denny's diet improves his health, what would you say then?"

"I . . . I don't know. . . ."

"Very well, then we shall see."

Three days had passed since that conversation, and Denny was decidedly better. This in itself was proof enough that someone had tried to poison him. She would speak to Reggie and see what he had to say now!

SEVEN

Plague take Brandy Fernwood! Cynthia Hayward nearly pulled at her long dark curls as she paced in the quiet of her chambers. Miss Fernwood was certainly upsetting all her dreams. And Sir Reginald? Yes, he posed a threat as well. Something had to be done!

Conscience? It pinched, but she shouted it down. There was Alistair to think of, Alistair to protect. Denny was so very much in the way, and now, now so was this Miss Fernwood!

It was a fact she would have to deal with sooner or later. But for now, there was something she could do immediately that would, she believed, successfully remove Sir Reginald from Lara's heart. At least, if not from her heart, then from her mind. It was why she had sent for Lara this morning. Yes, Lara had to be reminded.

A knock sounded, and a moment later Cynthia was pulling her door open, brushing aside the dark-brown velvet wrapper she had chosen to wear. "Lara . . . do come in."

Lara had a lace handkerchief in her hand. She twisted it but did as she was asked. What could this summons mean? What did her aunt want of her?

"Lara . . . do sit and be comfortable. I think the tea is still warm. Shall I pour you a cup?" She moved to the satinwood table holding the silver tray of tea and biscuits.

"No . . . no thank you." Lara put her hands in her lap. "What is it, Aunt Cynthia, that you wished to talk to me about?"

Cynthia Hayward frowned. "It is such a problem . . . I don't know what we should do. I think, however, that 'tis time we spoke of it, you and I."

"Spoke of it? What do you mean?" Lara eyed her fearfully. The last time she was put in this frame of mind, Cynthia had written to her in Brighton telling her of her father's death . . . and reminding her of her mother.

"Child . . . I am aware that Sir Reginald is . . . is becoming increasingly attached to you."

"No . . . no . . ."

"Yes, my dear, and it is not quite fair, is it?" She waited for Lara to look away. "Perhaps if you explained your circumstances to him he wouldn't mind?" This was a chance she had to take. Offer this up and then show Lara why it was so impossible.

82

"No! I don't want anyone to know." Lara lost all trace of color, so great was her agitation.

"I don't know that that is the wise course. Eventually Denny will have to be told."

"Not now. He is too young . . . too weak still. Please, Aunt Cynthia, Denny must not be told."

"But if you wish to encourage Sir Reginald," put in Cynthia slyly, for here was her thrust, "then Denny must be told, must be prepared for the inevitable news."

"I shan't encourage Sir Reginald. . . . Please, Aunt . . . let us drop the subject."

"You know, my dear . . . you should be thinking of marriage," returned Cynthia quietly.

"Should I? I don't think marriage at the present time is possible." Lara's voice was dull, devoid of passion.

"Alistair wants you to think of it. He has a decided tendre for you, my dear . . . and you know with Alistair, the secret of your mother would always be guarded."

"Yes, Alistair is very good. . . ." She rose from her chair. "If you will excuse me, Aunt Cynthia, I want to look in on Denny."

"That is another thing. How long does this Fernwood chit propose to remain in our household?"

Lara put up her chin. "Brandice is welcome here as long as she wishes to stay. You know, Aunt, Brandy's care of Denny has been wondrously beneficial."

"Has it, my dear? Dr. Franklin did say there might be a slight remission . . . and that you should not be hopeful because of it."

"Did he say that? I . . . I did not know." Lara was immediately cast down. She moved away without another word, and Cynthia allowed her to leave on this note.

In the hall, Lara met with Sir Reginald. He saw the paleness of her cheek and went to her at once.

"Lara . . . what is wrong?"

She cast fretful eyes at him. "Oh God . . . you should not have come. . . ." With which she dissolved into tears and ran to her room.

He was left standing in dejection. It was time to go to Brandy for help. He had not discussed the subject of Lara, for his cousin had had her hands full these past few days, but it could be put off no more! Purposefully he made his way to Brandy's room.

Brandy had already left her quarters, and found Denny in spirits and ready for some exercise. Hurriedly he rushed into his gray school clothes and followed her below to the library, where a bright fire burned. There they took out the pieces to Fox and Hound and proceeded to have a go at it with riotous rivalry.

"Oh you!" cried Denny merrily. "Don't think you can befuddle me, 'cause you can't, Brandy, and so I tell you!"

"Can't I just?" Brandy laughed. She was so pleased to see him lively again. His fair hair hung limply, a sign of his poor state of health, but he was no longer the dying little boy he had been only three days before. "In the meantime, my

84

little man, take a bit of your toast and apple . . . please."

As he complied with his goddess' wishes the library doors opened. In stepped Marden, unannounced. He stood for a moment, his eyes warming at the sight of Brandy on her knees. She had not done up her copper tresses and they fell about her shoulders in massive, silky profusion, glistening with the ray of sunlight that enveloped her. Her brown cambric swirled all around her feet. The ivory lace at her throat and cuffs made her seem so very young, as did her pose. Her eyes when she looked up to find him twinkled audaciously, and he felt his breath wrenched from him. "Well," he managed at last. "I find you up and very fine this morning, my lord Quendon." He made the lad a bow.

"Aye, come join us, Marden!" cried the boy joyously.

"I think not," retorted Marden. "Think of my dignity."

Brandy giggled. "Denny, think of his age!"

"My *age?*" Marden was taken aback but quickly recovered when he saw the laughter in her green eyes. She was a minx. "Never mind my age, but my tailor . . . I shudder to think what rebukes he would call down on my head if I were to crawl about the floor in his freshly cut breeches."

Brandy and Denny laughed, and Brandy allowed Lord Marden to give her a hand and help her up. Denny watched them a moment, sighed, and fell to playing by himself.

Marden's voice dropped as he walked with

Brandy towards the glass doors. "Why haven't you accepted at least one of my invitations to join your cousin for dinner with Fisk and myself?"

"I . . . I could not. . . ."

"Could not or would not, Miss Fernwood?" His tone was light, but there was an intenseness in his aqua eyes she could not put aside.

"Why, sir . . . could not, of course. I would have enjoyed a night out. . . . It has not been exactly the liveliest time of my life, these past three nights here, but I could not leave Lara to the company of her . . . relatives at such a time." She frowned at Marden. "You should not have taken Fisk and Reggie away from us!"

He laughed out loud. "Fisk, you know, was not about to spend another moment in this house after Denny fell ill. . . . And your cousin Reginald seems to be going through his own sort of hell." He took up her hand audaciously. "You should be very grateful to me, my dear."

She was disturbed by this last. "Reggie . . . is upset?" She shook her head. "I have been so caught up with Denny I did not notice." This was more to herself than to him.

He frowned. Something inside of him tugged, warned him not to get involved. And still his voice was assuaging, and finally he had the palm of her hand opened, and traced the lines of it with his ungloved finger. "Brandy . . . whether Lara joins or no, come have dinner with us tonight. Bring Denny. It will be a treat for him, and in his honor we shall dine early."

Denny heard this and jumped to his feet to add

his entreaty to Kurt Marden's. "Yes, Brandy . . . it is only fair, for I have been good, haven't I? Please, Brandy . . ."

"Oh, Denny . . . I don't know that Lara will agree. You know she doesn't really approve of his lordship. . . ."

"Oh, posh!" returned Denny.

"Exactly so, posh," agreed Marden with a grin. "I am a perfectly respectable nobleman."

"Well . . . if we don't stay too long . . . and if you promise to take a nice long nap this afternoon, Denny, for you are not yet strong and I don't want to overexert you."

"Brandy, I promise, I do."

She turned to Marden, "Very well then, sir, I do believe you have two new guests."

He now kissed her palm. "So I do, and, my beauty, I count it a start."

At that she realized that her hand had been pleasurably in his hold and withdrew it immediately. He was an arrogant blade, was this Marden. She had just better watch herself lest she allow his flirtation to go to her head.

Sir Reginald exploded into the library. He had not found Brandy in her room. Further inquiry had elicited the information that she had gone with Denny to the library, and in some frustration he followed. Upon finding Marden present there as well, he ran his hand through his fair hair and said on an anguished note, "Marden . . . I'm glad you are here. I shall be returning with you to Marden Towers."

"Will you, old boy? What's towards?" said Marden

on a quiet note. It was obvious his friend was in dire straits.

"I . . . I can't explain now . . . nor do I wish to. Am I welcome?"

"Of course, you fool. Welcome indeed," returned Marden putting a hand on his shoulder.

"What is this?" cried Brandy. "Reg . . . what is the matter?"

He fidgeted. "I need to talk to you . . . in private, Brandy. . . ." he looked towards Marden.

"Of course. I will take Denny for a stroll with me about the garden. Eh, Denny, are you game?" Marden put in amicably.

"Aye, that I am. I'll just get my coat."

"I'll come with you." And with this he and Denny left Sir Reginald to his cousin.

"Now," said Brandy firmly, "explain yourself."

"I . . . I don't know where to begin. Brandy . . . Lara won't have me. It's no different than it was last month . . . but you were right about one thing. She is not indifferent to my suit."

"Ah, I thought you and Lara had begun to reach an understanding. I am so sorry, Reg," said Brandy sympathetically.

"No . . . the night of the carnival she repeated what she told me a month ago. She will not marry me. Said something stupid about its having to do with her father's death. She seems to think that marrying me would somehow interfere with her responsibilities."

"That doesn't make any sense."

"Precisely. That is why I need you to talk to her.

Get her to explain what she means by such an absurd statement."

"Reggie ... my friendship with Lara is not based on prying," Brandy said gravely.

"Prying? I haven't asked you to pry, only to see if she won't confide in you, talk to you. . . ."

Brandy sighed. "Well it is obvious that something is troubling Lara, and it is more than her father's death and Denny's illness. Yes, I will feel her out and see what she will tell me."

He took up her hand and put it to his lips. "Brandy, you are the best of good friends."

Marden chose this auspicious moment to reenter the library. He was startled by the vision that met his aqua eyes. He had not previously supposed that Sir Reginald might be a suitor for Brandy's hand. He found the suspicion strangely disquieting.

"Well, Reg ... I must leave. Do you come with me?"

"Yes," he answered hastily. "You understand . . . don't you, Brandy?"

"Of course. Shall I send your things to you?"

"If you would."

"Done." She looked again at Marden. Why was his mouth set so sternly? "Where, my lord, has Denny gone off to?"

"I sent him to the schoolroom. There is a great deal he must catch up with if he is to return to Eton next month."

She smiled warmly. "Thank you."

He inclined his head. "You have no need to thank me. I had Denny's interests in mind at the

89

time—however, as it has served to please you, *I* am thankful."

"A very pretty speech. Careful, my lord, any more like that and I might take it into my head to think you a very good sort of fellow," she bantered.

"And why should you not?"

"Because it would so soil your evil reputation." She laughed and waved them off. After they had gone she stood a moment. Reggie was quite right. Lara needed a talking to, even at the risk of delving where she did not belong. Purposefully, she made for Lara's room.

EIGHT

Deana Hopkins fingered the selection of pink and white flowers she had cut in the hothouse as she made her way across the lawns to the front doors of the Abbey. A gust of wind caught the hood of her dark cloak and swept it aside. Her short dark curls swirled in the wind, and with an inaudible oath, she pulled the hood back onto her head. At the same time she looked up to find Lord Marden and Sir Reginald on their way past her towards the stables. They stopped and tipped their hats.

She smiled flirtatiously. "Good morning, gentlemen. Where are you off to . . . some odious cockfight?"

"No! By Jove, Miss Hopkins, is there one in the neighborhood?" asked Sir Reginald hopefully.

She laughed amicably enough. "I have not the slightest idea."

"What lovely flowers," observed Lord Marden quietly. He cast her a smile, inviting her to elaborate on the subject.

"Yes . . . they are mums, you know. I've picked them for my aunt. She has been poorly out of spirits with Alistair away these past three days."

"Oh? I wasn't aware that Mr. Hayward was away from the estate," returned Marden interestedly.

She frowned lest anyone misunderstand and think Hayward was taking some sort of holiday, "Yes, he is away on business . . . for the estate, you know. Denny Quendon is very fortunate to have so conscientious an agent in his cousin." She bit her lip. Had she perhaps said too much?

"Miss Hopkins," called Lord Marden as an afterthought.

"Y-es?" She turned back towards him.

"I have invited Miss Fernwood and Denny to be our guests tonight at the Towers for an early dinner. As Lara and Mrs. Hayward are still not accepting invitations, I thought perhaps you might like to join us?"

"Oh no . . . I am, you know, part of the family . . . and it would not be right . . ."

"Oh . . . do come," put in Sir Reginald. "After all, you cannot be expected to mourn more than a month. You are but a connection only . . . and you will be nice company for Brandy on the ride over to the Towers."

"Oh? Don't you join?" she was surprised.

"Well . . . as to that, I shall be awaiting you at

the Towers. I am leaving Quendon Abbey . . . and taking up residence with Fisk and Marden here," said Sir Reginald quietly.

"I see. Well, I shall ask my aunt what she thinks and send a message over with my answer later in the day." She smiled. "In the meantime, enjoy yourselves, gentlemen." She moved away.

"We shall try," returned Marden, watching her go off. Then to Sir Reginald who had fallen to brooding. "Attractive female, that. I wonder how it is she buries herself here at Quendon?"

"Hmmm? Oh yes. . . ." agreed Sir Reginald absently.

"Of course, she is nothing to Miss Fernwood. Beautiful, your cousin," further pursued Marden, interested now to understand where Sir Reginald's thoughts were.

"Fine girl, Brandy. The best, in fact," returned Sir Reginald.

Lord Marden's brow went up. Was that how the wind blew? Was Sir Reginald finding himself in dire straits over Brandy? And even if it was so, why should it so nettle him? Why should he care if Brandy and her cousin were about to make a match of it? Why indeed?

Brandy discovered that Lara would not admit her to her room. She stood without, knocking and begging admittance, but Lara called out that she wanted to get some sleep. Somewhat out of patience with her friend, Brandy scooped up her cloak and made for the stables. However, she got to the front door and found herself facing **Deana Hopkins.**

"Oh . . . Miss Hopkins . . ." She saw the basket of flowers. "What lovely blooms. From the hothouse?"

"Where else?" returned Miss Hopkins curtly. She had no liking for Brandy. The girl didn't belong here. She was far too beautiful, and Alistair had paid her far too much attention at dinner the night before he left. Then too, she interfered with Denny more than was right. After all, she was an outsider, wasn't she?

She had enough competition with Lara; she didn't need this beautiful heiress throwing herself at Alistair! She brushed past Brandy.

Brandy was surprised and just a little hurt by Deana Hopkins. She had been attempting friendship since her arrival, but the girl would have none of her. She felt like retorting that there were mums of various sizes and colors growing in flower beds all over the park grounds, but she restrained herself. Instead she attempted another overture at friendship.

"I was about to take my mare out for some exercise. Would you care to join me for a ride?"

"Thank you, no," answered the girl, continuing on her way and not bothering to make an excuse.

Brandy lost her temper. "Too bad, but then I don't imagine you have bottom enough to keep up."

Deana turned, glared, and looked as though she might retort. However, she was quick to understand the sparring gleam in Brandy's eyes. Here was a worthy opponent. Save it. Yes indeed, she would save it.

Brandy stomped out of the house. Everyone in it was crazy. Even her friend Lara was going noddy on her. What was wrong with Lara? The girl should be blissful at Denny's upstroke in health.

She tacked up her mare, nimbly climbed into the saddle, spread her skirts around herself, and sent the mare forward into a trot. They took the path that led to the fields, and she broke into a canter, hand galloped, collected the mare for the fence, and took her over neatly. Another field was spanned before Brandy was feeling herself again.

An hour later she was undoing the girth, lifting off the saddle, sliding it onto the rack, rubbing down the mare, and talking to her all the while. "You don't know, do you, Brown Sugar? Of course you don't. How could you know, when I don't?"

"What don't you know?" asked a familiar male voice.

Brandy spun around and found Alistair Hayward grinning provocatively at her. Some days ago Alistair had realized that Brandy was not only beautiful, she was also an heiress. There was no saying what that could develop into.

"Hallo! Welcome back," cried Brandy sincerely. She rather liked Alistair Hayward. He was a fine-looking man. He was charming and soft-spoken.

"Thank you. Now, what is it that you and your mare don't know?" He was teasing her.

She sighed. "A great many things."

He touched her nose, and his tone grew more serious. "Ah, little pretty, I've missed you these days."

This was forward indeed. She stepped back an inch, for handsome as he was she was not about to let any man take such a heady liberty. "I trust, sir, that your expedition was a successful one?"

He knew well enough when to retreat. "Little Lord Quendon will benefit from it, if that is what you mean." He sounded very much on the defensive.

"Oooh? Don't you bite my head off too."

He laughed. "Has someone already snipped at you?"

"Yes indeed. I think I must be fair game this morning, but never mind, I rode off my feisty mood with Brown Sugar." She stepped away from her handiwork and left the mare in her stall.

He led her outside, "Only tell me who has had a go at you, love, and I'll have his head!" said he gallantly.

She giggled. "I am persuaded you would not." There was a tease in her eyes.

He opened his marsh-brown eyes wide. "Who, then? Never say you are at odds with m'mother?" He suspicioned that this was so, for before his departure his mother had already expressed the desire to be rid of Miss Fernwood.

"Your mother? Why no, she is always pleasant to me, though in truth I think she wishes me at Jericho."

"No, you must not think that. It is just that she is so worried about Denny . . . about Lara . . ."

"Yes, of course, and here I am popping in on her with solutions she finds suspicious. No, I can understand that." She wondered for a moment if she could. Wasn't everyone in the household held in suspicion? Wasn't even Hayward here? After all, Denny did get better . . . but then Hayward had been away. . . .

He frowned. She was going off into another realm. He could sense it, and he strove to bring her back to himself. "So then, Miss Fernwood, who did get you all . . . er . . . feisty, this morning?"

The door was opened wide by Jeffreys, who had seen them walking up the drive. As they stepped within they were met by Deana, who was dressed for riding in an old dark-blue wool riding habit. She swung a crop in her hand but checked when she saw the arrivals. Her expression of joyful welcome flitted into chagrin when she observed that Alistair was accompanied by Brandy.

Brandy noted this at once and could not help a tease. "Oh, changed your mind, Miss Hopkins?"

"Y-es . . ." She turned to Alistair and went onto tiptoes to put a soft peck upon his cheek. "Welcome home, cousin," she said softly.

"Thank you, Deana. You are looking well." He was playing a complex game. His intentions were to court both Lara and Brandy without either one realizing this. However, Deana would see all, and she could be a nuisance.

"Enjoy yourself, Miss Hopkins," said Brandy, more brightly, more sweetly than she felt.

Deana cast her a hard glance, smiled again at Alistair, and was gone. Brandy moved towards the stairs. "Till later, sir. There is a young man I want to look in on." It had occurred to her that he had not yet asked about Denny, and this she found somewhat surprising.

"How does our young lord go on?" he asked solicitously.

"Better, sir, much, much better." With this she skipped lightly out of his sight. She wished she knew who was responsible for Denny's wretched condition. Alistair? Mrs. Hayward? Never Lara . . . no, not Lara . . . but she was the one to gain, wasn't she? Well, devil take all other considerations. She was going to find out!

Purposefully she made towards Lara's door. Whether her friend was willing or not, she meant to enter and have a word or two with her!

NINE

The evening showed promise. The men at Marden Towers were all moved to admiration when Brandy entered. She was looking ravishing in an exquisite gown of forest-green silk. Its cut was fashionably low, its waistline high, its line clinging to the ankles of her dainty feet. Her copper tresses were piled in curls upon her head and cascaded in profusion down her back. Here and there small green leaves peeped between the fiery curls. At her ears were emeralds and pearls, and the same encircled her fine neck.

Deana had not chosen to join them, and so it was that Brandy found herself with only Denny as chaperon between her three male hosts. This in itself purported entertainment, for Brandy could see they were all well disposed to please. However, then entered yet another bachelor on their scene.

Mr. John Kingston, comptroller of stamps for the Cotswolds region, had reason to be grateful to Lord Marden, for his lordship had extended Kingston's family several courtesies while in London. However, the two had never met. Kingston had been in the area staying with friends and thought he would on his way home make a quick stop for perhaps high tea and pay his respects to Marden.

Kingston found upon his intrusion that Marden was gracious enough to extend to him an invitation to join the dinner party. Kingston did not approve of early dining; however, he accepted the invitation out of a sense of civility.

The assembled dinner group made room for the new arrival at the table and discovered that the gentleman had unlimited prose at his disposal. However, here and there Marden or Reg was able to interject an interesting subject, and it was upon Castlereagh that Marden brought down a smarting word.

"It isn't so, Reg. I tell you that we have nothing but the yell for war and Castlereagh is preparing his head for the pike, on which we shall see it carried before he has done."

To this, Kingston astounded the company by interjecting, "An interesting city is Milan. I enjoyed my travels there immensely. I say, Marden, were you not in Milan some years ago?"

All eyes went from Marden to Kingston and then back again to Marden. "I . . . was there," said Marden, his brows drawn in puzzlement.

Fisk leaned over and said to Sir Reginald, "Who is this fool?"

"Shh," ordered Reg, and then brought him into the conversation. "You were there with Marden, weren't you, Fisk?"

Kingston did not wait for Fisk's reply but proceeded thoughtfully and in his monotone, "Did you happen to find Carlo Boromeo while you were there? Fascinating creature."

Fisk shook his head, "No . . . never met the fellow, did we, Marden?"

Kingston looked surprised. "No, no, he is dead, you know. Preserved. A very fine dead body he is."

Fisk brought up his quizzing glass to study the man. Denny nearly choked on his food and Brandy sought refuge in her hand. Sir Reggie dove under the table, presumably to fetch his napkin, and only Marden was able to preserve his demeanor.

Some time later they had retired to the parlor, which was decorated in hues of green and white and elicited the remark from Kingston that he rather thought it made him feel as though he were in a box of lilies. Fisk again raised his quizzing glass.

"Ever been in a box of lilies?" asked Fisk.

"No," said Kingston.

"How do you know what it feels like?"

"One imagines, you know," replied Kingston.

"This one doesn't . . . at least not about lilies," stated Fisk, taking a long pull of his port and settling by the fire.

Kingston sighed and moved to the hearth, applied a log to its already high flame, and swayed to and fro at its base. Brandy contemplated him as he stood there. He was something of a dandy. His shirt points were exaggeratedly high and prevented him from turning his head in either direction. His waistcoat was a bright collection of stripes, and his coattails were wondrously long.

Suddenly a crackle and pop at his back found its mark and began eating away at his coattail. The flame grew, and Brandy jumped to her feet with a start. "Fire!" she cried in some distress.

Marden saw at once that it was his guest who was on fire and rushed to put it out. Denny knew that water would help and took out a pretty assortment of flowers from their vase and dashed into the fray. However, he had to stand there and take aim, for by this time Kingston was running about in a circle trying to put out his fire and everyone was yelling advice. Finally he got his chance, and swish, the fire was out, and Kingston was nicely drenched.

He waited till he could get his breath before he politely thanked young Lord Quendon for his assistance and apologized for his early departure.

"I fear I must go and change," he explained. "Must see I can't stand here . . . in such a condition with a lady present."

They agreed to it and some moments later fell into indecent mirth. Denny declared that it had been a bang-up good evening and Brandy reluctantly said it was time she saw him home. "We don't want to overdo. . . ."

Their carriage was called for, and Brandy stepped into the hall to receive her dark velvet cloak. Marden took it from his lackey and draped it over her shoulders. His touch caused her to tremble, and in some idiotish confusion she glanced around and found his eyes. There was an expression there that warmed her blood, and quietly, almost inaudibly, she thanked him for an enjoyable evening.

"The pleasure was all mine." The urge to brush her lips with his own was almost overwhelming. He had to straighten quickly, to pull away or yield to impulse.

She misconstrued, and her little chin went up. "I am only sorry that Miss Hopkins was not able to accept your invitation. I am certain you missed her company tonight."

Was she piqued? The notion amused him, delighted him. "I would have found Miss Hopkins presence here . . . enlightening, but it was yours I found necessary."

The coach arrived, and Denny pulled her along towards its doors. It occurred to her that one of these fine men should have at least offered to ride home with her, but never mind, it seemed chivalry was dead.

The three gentlemen did, however, accompany her outside to the waiting coach and saw her comfortably within. Denny clambered in beside her and told them all not to worry, he would take care of Brandy on the way home.

Sir Reginald buckled his lips, and as he saw Fisk about to open his mouth at this juncture, took the liberty of giving his friend a gentle kick at his ankle. Fisk glared at Reg but made no verbal protest. Thus it was they stood with Marden and waved the carriage off. However, once it was out of earshot, Reginald did turn a frown on Marden.

"Lord, Kurt . . . don't understand why you didn't let one of us offer to escort them home." He shook his head. "Don't like the idea of them on the road alone at this hour."

" 'Tis not late," said Marden curtly, "and I have my reasons. Now why don't you go on . . . get back into the house. I'll be with you directly."

Fisk started up the stone steps, but Reg considered Marden a long moment. "What's this, my lord . . . just what are you up to that you are not letting us in on?" His formality indicated that his bristles were on end.

Marden laughed. "Come out of the boughs, my friend, you will know soon enough. Now . . . go on, I shan't be long." With this he turned and made for the stables.

Inside the carriage, Brandy felt along the back wall for the lever to the secret compartment. Sir Reginald's mother always used it when traveling any distance to conceal valuables. Brandy's gloved hand sought inside the dropleaf drawer within and found the smooth metal object and brought it out and laid it in her lap. Denny eyed the lady's gun with excitement.

"Grand! Lord, Brandy, if you aren't the most complete hand!" He shook his head in open admiration. "Not like a girl at all." He had in his estimation paid her the highest-ranking compliment.

She laughed lightly and pulled the blue top hat he wore over his forehead. "And you are the most complete gamin! Not like a girl indeed."

He chuckled and pushed his hat back and away from his forehead so that it sat rakishly on his fair curls. "But Brandy ... will we need it, do you think?"

She eyed him. He was looking so much better. "Do you know, Denny, that in no time at all you are going to have all the girls swooning at your feet?"

"Aw ... go on." He flushed and returned tenaciously to the subject at hand. "Brandy ... if you brought that thing"—he pointed at the small gun—"you must have thought we might need it."

She had brought out the diminutive weapon from her trunk and concealed it in the coach before they had left for Marden Towers. Why? She repeatedly asked herself why. The answer finally came in a flood: because things were not as they should be. Denny was eleven years old. He was a lord and he was master of some sizable estates and fortune, and he was a target for murder. An ugly word, but a genuine possibility all the same. There was no sense stretching his neck over the block by taking him out into the open at night; there could be a danger in that. After all, he had survived the poison, and it would be obvious now to the individual who was behind it that Brandy was not about to allow such a thing to be administered to him again. Thus he could be in danger by other means. She slid the gun into her cloak pocket. Instinct had moved her, but logic reaffirmed the correctness of her actions.

"There is never any saying," she answered Denny

at last for he repeated his question. "Now tell me how you enjoyed your evening out."

He sighed pleasurably. "Oh, Brandy . . . when Fisk kept bending to me and mumbling about Kingston I thought I would laugh out loud."

"Terrible child. It isn't nice to laugh at your elders!" teased Brandy.

"Oh, but Brandy, only wait till you hear what Fisk said about him."

"What did he say to you about poor Mr. Kingston?"

"He leaned into me and said, 'He seems a silly fellow . . . forever prosing on . . . what? What did the silly fellow say now?' And then, Brandy, he would put up his quizzing glass and stare so. I nearly came undone, and then when Kingston stuck in at dinner about that mummy being a fine dead body I thought Fisk would go off into an apoplexy! Lord, *I* almost did."

Brandy chuckled sweetly in tune to Denny's laughter, but the sound quickly died in her throat. She could see two dark figures on horseback. They were coming across the field, cutting the carriage's horses off, leveling their pistols. The coach came to a lurching halt. The horses snorted, whinnied, and restlessly threw about their heads in nervous agitation. The report of a gun confirmed Brandy's fears. She heard them growl a threat. Loud and sure they were, these two. The driver of their coach sat rigid, for there was no doubt. *Highwaymen!*

TEN

Brandy's hand slid into her velvet-lined pocket. she looked around at Denny beside her. His hat had fallen off and his face was taut, drawn in fear. However, the brave lad patted her knee and reassured her.

"Don't worry, Brandy . . . I shall defend you. Best give over the gun."

"Shhh, darling. Say nothing to these men and give over whatever trinkets they may ask for."

"But . . ." he objected.

"Trust me, Denny, please."

The door of the carriage was swung wide, and a man both large and heavy, covered in black from head to toe, stood before them. Only the glinting eyes were visible beneath the cloth that hung over his head. His voice came muffled but loud and ominous.

"Get out!"

"How dare you speak to a lady like that!" cried Denny in as deep a voice as he could muster.

The man laughed and yanked at Denny's collar, dragging the boy out of the carriage roughly.

"Little snit! If ye know what is best fer ye, ye'll keep yer mouth shut!"

"Put him over the saddle and let's be gone!" cried the other man, who held his cohort's horse and his own in tow and leveled a gun at the driver with his free hand.

Brandy had jumped out of the carriage and surveyed the situation. Somehow she had to get herself between these two men, get Denny out of their reach. But how?

The moon's rays glistened on his gun. He held Denny with a tight grip, and the boy squealed, kicked, and fought frantically to get free. She had to do something quickly.

She put a hand to her hip, brushing part of her cloak aside, as she smiled coquettishly at the man holding Denny.

"Sir . . ." Her voice came sultry soft, arresting, and she was pleased to find that he gave her his full attention. Denny too stopped his wiggling to see what Brandy was at. "I am certain we have no quarrel with you." She was close enough now for the man to smell her perfume. "You want your evening's work to be profitable . . . and I have the means . . ."

"Eh? I don't get your drift."

"Highwaymen must have their sparklers . . . their cash. I haven't any cash, sir . . . but I do have

108

a ring to make your evening worth the trouble." She removed her hand from its pocket and at the same time grabbed hold of Denny and pulled him roughly out of his attacker's grip. She thrust him behind her, simultaneously raising her weapon to point at the toby's head and taking a step out of his reach.

He released an oath and waved his horse pistol around. Demme, how could he have let her get the better of him that way? However, he looked at her gun derisively and released a chortle of laughter.

"Well now, mort . . . what be yer purpose wit' that toy?"

She answered sweetly, "I can, sir, put a neat little hole through your head. True now, it's not as big and bold as the gun you wave at me, but I do assure you it can do the job for me."

Warily he eyed her. "Aye . . . and me man up yonder"—he indicated with a jerk of his head—"he could serve ye much the same."

"You would still be dead. Very dead."

"Would I now? Might be I'll 'ave to risk that, seeing as I 'ave a rig to do." He moved towards her menacingly.

Lord Marden saddled his own horse and at some distance followed the carriage home. This was probably absurd, but more and more he was beginning to believe that Denny Quendon was in mortal danger. He had not allowed either Reg or Fisk to ride home with the carriage because he hadn't felt either man would have adequately attended the situation. Sir Reg, he knew, did not really believe in Brandy's suspicions, and Fisk was certainly not the man for this particular errand. He settled it in his mind to follow the coach home.

Hayward was back from his trip, and Hayward stood to gain by Denny's demise, for Marden had made some discreet inquiries and discovered the next in line for the Quendon inheritance was Alistair Hayward!

He saw the high tobies. One stood holding the reins of two horses and leveled a gun at the driver, who sat mutely. The other was waving a gun at Brandy, gripping Denny with his other hand. He saw Brandy suddenly lunge and put the boy behind her. He saw her aim her small gun at the highwayman's head. Damn but she seemed capable of anything. He undid his gun from its holder.

There is an unmistakable sound a horse makes when it is tearing up earth. It digs into the turf and throws it away, it thunders across ground, it tears into the wind, and then does a man know speed. Such is a horse's full gallop.

Marden's dapple gray's neck was stretched out ahead as he charged the scene. The two highwaymen looked up at the undeniable sound, struck for a moment into dull stupidity.

"Hell and Brimstone, Tally!" cried the brute holding the horses. He was already scrambling into his saddle. "Let's get out of 'ere!"

Tally cursed out loud, but a shot chanced to whiz too close to his unshaven cheek. Nothing had gone right this evening. Here was a rider, charging and shooting at 'em . . . and here too some slip

110

of a chit looking like she would be pleased enough to put a hole in his head! Hastily he followed his partner and took off. This was one rig he'd have to mark up as a loss!

The two highwaymen took off speedily just as Marden slowed his gray and had them neatly in his line of fire. His lordship released another shot, and they heard one of the men cry out in pain. However, neither of the tobies slowed, and soon the darkness had them well hidden.

Marden reined in his animal to a complete stop and jumped hurriedly down to take up Brandy's shoulders in a tight scoop.

"Have they harmed you, sweetheart?" His eyes anxiously appraised her, and before her reply was out he had his answer and relaxed.

"Not in the least," she answered breathlessly, for his touch sent shivers through her body. It was ridiculous . . . and it was ridiculous that he should call her sweetheart! He was too free with his manners, this one, but still this was no time to call him out on the point. Instead, she did otherwise. "That was prodigiously well done, my lord. The way you handled your animal, yourself . . . and still managed to get off those shots . . . well, you were quite wonderful!"

He laughed. "I must say much the same for you, love." He touched the gun she still held in her hand. "Do you always travel so well armed?" Never before had he seen her like, and for some irrational reason it exhilarated him.

"No, not always," she answered on a more subdued note. Love . . . he used the word too freely. Had he no depth?

"Lord Marden," cried Denny, bringing some attention to himself, "you should have seen her. She aimed her little gun right at that man's head and promised to blow a hole right through him."

Marden and Brandy laughed, and she said, "You weren't so bad yourself, my little lord. I seem to remember you kicking the poor brute enough to give him a sore memory of this night for some time to come!"

Denny acknowledged this proudly, and then Marden was taking over, ushering the boy into the carriage, seeing the lad within, and then turning to Brandy.

"Come, Miss Fernwood . . . the night air is damp. . . ."

"So solicitous, my lord," she returned quietly, consideringly, as she gazed up at his aqua eyes. Quickly she plunged on before his disarming glance made her forget her purpose. "Tell me, Lord Marden, why did you end in following us tonight?"

"Follow you? I don't understand," he said easily.

She frowned and nearly stamped her foot. "I am no fool, my lord. Please do not insult my intelligence!"

He grinned. "I wouldn't dream of it . . . especially while you still brandish that weapon, Miss Fernwood."

So, he was back to Miss Fernwood, and rightly so. Nonetheless, it rather nettled her. She stuffed the gun back into her cloak's side pocket and pursued tenaciously, "My lord, do you suspect

112

someone of trying to harm Denny? Is that why you followed us home? Is it?" Her voice was low, tense, for she did not wish the lad to hear. She could see him reclining in the coach, with his head back and his eyes closed. Without realizing it, she had moved closer to Kurt Marden so that they could speak without Denny's overhearing.

He put his finger to her chin. "You are allowing your imagination to upset you, Miss Fernwood. These scoundrels were highwaymen . . . nothing more." His gentle scoff did not, however, mollify her, and he opened his eyes wide as she glared at him. Devil was in it that she was far too beautiful and much too near!

"Stuff!" was her unladylike reply. "Highwaymen they may be, my lord, but their purpose with us was not to run off with our valuables! They had no interest in such things. I tell you they wanted Denny." She found his nearness disconcerting and took a step backwards.

He moved towards her, directing her purposely at the boot at the back of the coach. "Did they, Miss Fernwood?" His tone was gentle, assuaging. He took up her elbow, for he meant to see her inside the coach before the discussion went any further.

"Do *not* patronize me, sir!" She pulled out of his hold and started to stomp off in something of a huff.

He should let her go. She would get into the carriage and he would see them home without any further delving into the dangerous subject. Logic told him this, and yet he reached out and caught

113

her wrist, spun her around, and had her neatly planted against the boot of the carriage.

Brandy flushed in the darkness and glared daringly up into his aqua eyes. She could feel the driver straining around to look at them, but they were not in his line of vision, and she knew that Marden was aware of this. She felt her blood surge through her body. She felt herself grow warm with a desire she blushed to own. His ungloved hands took up her arms; she could feel his fingers grip through the material of her cloak, through her gown, and her flesh felt singed.

"Ah, spitfire," he whispered as his mouth sought and found her own.

She pushed ineffectually against his chest for a moment. There was no resisting his kiss. It touched a portal never opened before and unlocked its latch. How dare he? railed her mind, and still did she return his kiss. She heard him whisper her name.

"Brandy . . . such a beauteous Brandy wine . . ."

It thrilled her. His voice swept away so many considerations, but she wasn't going to allow this, she must not allow this. Something inside of her called him to order, and he heard it in her voice.

"My lord . . . please . . . stop, you . . . take advantage. . . ."

He drew himself up and gazed at her long. "Come, sweetheart, do not expect me to apologize. I cannot, for I do not in the least regret it. Do you?"

She brought around her open hand, but he caught it and prevented the blow. His smile she

114

found strangely tender, incongruous with his present behavior.

"Come then, Miss Fernwood, do forgive me. . . . After all, 'twas just a bit of payment for my daring rescue."

She put up her chin. "Please let me go, my lord."

He dropped his arms to his side and stepped out of her path. She moved off but found him opening the carriage door, helping her within. She sat back, but as he closed the door he said quietly, "Ah, sweetheart, would that I could allay your fears. Can you not trust me and avoid taking unnecessary risks?"

Quietly she answered, "Trust you? But I just did, my lord . . . and see how I was answered. Risks, my lord? But you said there are none beyond my imagination."

"But the imagination, especially yours, seems to be enough to worry you. I would that you would calm yourself."

"I am calm, my lord. I am also wary. It serves," she answered curtly.

He refrained from retorting, for it seemed Miss Fernwood was as headstrong as she was brave. Instead he answered, "I shall follow the carriage until you are safely within your own grounds."

She only nodded her head to this and then resolutely looked away from him. Denny had in his sleep slipped into a position that was sure to give him a stiff neck. She pulled the boy so that his head fell into her lap, and then she sat to mull over her thoughts.

*   *   *

Some time later that night she lay awake in her bed, staring at the intricate moldings over her four-poster. It was an ornate ceiling, and she attempted to focus her thoughts on its design and forget Lord Marden's outrageous behavior. He had kissed her!

Now, what was in that to overset you? You have been kissed before. You have had three London seasons and some very notorious rakes have attempted much the same . . . and before you always laughed. Why are you so very upset by this Marden, by his kiss?

He is a rake! He flaunts his arrogance! He . . . he thinks he can do as he pleases! I will not have it . . . and he will not believe me. No one believes me. Denny is the target for murder, and not even Reggie will believe me!

Lara had not been any help. She had attempted to see Lara that afternoon, for Reggie's sake, knowing that Reggie would be anxiously awaiting some news when she came to dinner that evening, but Lara had refused to allow her admittance to her room. She had stood outside Lara's room and begged to enter, and Lara had only sobbed her away.

"But dearest," said Brandy to the door, "wouldn't you like to accompany us to Lord Marden's this evening? Reggie will be there."

"Please, Brandie . . . I am tired . . . I just want to rest," Lara cried softly on the other side of the door.

"Won't you let me come in for just a moment, Lara?"

116

"Later . . . not now. . . ."

Brandy had given up then, but would not do so again. No, definitely now Lara had to be faced with what was happening right in her own home. Denny was not only Lara's brother, he was her ward. She owed him some protection. Brandy was going to see to it that Lara woke up to her responsibilities. Indeed, come the morning, she and Lara were going to have it out. Then too there was the problem of Reg. It was just possible that the way Lara was behaving to Reg might have something to do with Denny!

She had told Reggie that she did not like to pry, but it was becoming apparent that that was exactly what she was going to have to do! Denny . . . Denny was in real danger.

Brandy clicked off her facts, touching her fingers as she did so. Three days Alistair Hayward had been gone. Alistair Hayward. Tall, weathered, good-looking Alistair Hayward. He had an engaging smile, a soft manner . . . and an ambition? What if he did have an ambition? Why should he not?

Alistair Hayward had been gone three days, and in those three days Denny's health had improved in great measure. Alistair Hayward had come home this day and in the same evening they had been attacked by highwaymen. Coincidence! Even a fool would see that would lend suspicion to himself. But no, they were highwaymen, only highwaymen.

Stuff and nonsense! Hired villains to abduct Denny, that is what they were, and if no one else would admit it, she knew it! Clearly she had heard one of them call out to put the boy over the saddle and be gone. That was all they wanted. Denny had been their game. Why hadn't Marden believed her? Why didn't Reggie see? Was it possible that she had concocted all this in her mind? Was she fitting events to a tale of her own making? Could she be wrong?

No. She was not wrong. Morning would hold some answers. Morning, and how she wished it were already. It was taking so long and there were so many things that needed to be investigated. Denny . . . his name drifted by her mind as she began to doze off. Denny. Denny. Denny. Over and over again she saw his face, heard his boyish, gleeful laughter, and then something ominous was moving towards him. Something without shape or voice. Something dark!

With a start she sat bolt upright. It was only a nightmare. It was only a fear manifesting itself in her dream. But suddenly she had to be up and see Denny for herself. She groped around the corner of her high mattress for her wrapper, found it, and slipped it on. She moved in the darkness to her nightstand and lit her candle in its small pewter holder before hurrying across her room to her hall door. Shivers of dread slid up and down her spine. Something was wrong. She could feel it in her bones. She had to get to Denny!

ELEVEN

Brandy quickly, stealthily sped down the long wide hallway to Denny's quarters. She quietly opened his door and had started to enter when a dark, tall, shadowy thing at the foot of Denny's bed sent her free hand to her heart and won a startled gasp from her.

The figure did not move at her entrance until Brandy shoved her candle in front of her and discovered the name to the lone creature. "Mrs Hayward . . . whatever are you doing here?"

Denny lay sleeping peacefully in his bed, and she seemed as though she were doing no more than contemplating his youthful beauty. She turned and cast indignant eyes upon the intruder.

"I was checking on my nephew, Miss Fernwood."

"Checking on him? Why? Did he cry out? What happened?" Brandy was nonplussed by the woman.

"If you must know," said Mrs. Hayward, wrapping her dark-brown robe about herself as though suddenly chilled, "Lara gave him a glass of warm milk and asked him to drink it before he went to sleep. I wanted to see if he had obeyed her."

Brandy's eyes flew to the nightstand, and it was with tremendous relief that she saw there a full glass of milk. Then her brow went up as she watched Mrs. Hayward glide towards the object in question and take it up.

"I see, Miss Fernwood, that his attachment to you is strong. He advised his sister that though it came from her own hands, he could not drink it. He said to her that even his dinner tonight was supervised by you."

"That is correct, Mrs. Hayward. Lord Marden was good enough to allow me my whims."

"I don't know why it is you should expect an explanation from me, but if you must have one, it so happens that Lara has been unwell most of the day. I looked in on her earlier, and she had mentioned to me that Denny had refused to drink the milk she brought him. She had been too tired to return it to the kitchens and didn't want to rouse any of the servants at that hour. It bothered me as I lay in bed. I knew it would go sour." She was moving towards the door. "So I just thought I would fetch it and feed it to my cat, Tabby."

"Of course," said Brandy absently. She was concentrating on the glass of milk. Here was Mrs. Hayward gliding away with the evidence. Arsenic? Could it be traced in the milk? Stop it! Now you are getting out of hand, she told herself. Lara gave that milk to Denny! Would Lara be putting arsenic in Denny's milk?

Yet here was Cynthia Hayward, gliding away with it. If there had been poison in the milk . . . could Mrs. Hayward be involved? Was she protecting herself or her son?

Alistair pulled Deana's muslin wrap around her tightly. She pressed herself against his bare chest. He frowned and stroked her head. Deana had taken things too far. He had been surprised earlier that night when he had opened his door to the knocking and found her standing there in her nightdress. Her dark short curls alluringly framed her face, and he knew himself stirred.

She had come to him, and he had had no resistance then, but now, now all his future plans shot up before his eyes and bittered the moment. Deana was complicating matters. What if their intimacy resulted in getting her with child? No. This was dangerous, and he had no wish to hurt Deana. She was a warm, loving creature, and though she moved him, he did not love her. Neither did he wish to hurt her. Hurt her? Had he not already done that? But it wasn't his fault. She had come to him . . . and he was only flesh and blood, after all!

He took up her shoulders roughly, for he was irritated with the situation as it now stood.

"Listen to me, Deana . . . what happened tonight was a mistake. It can't happen again." Then more gently, "I am sorry."

She looked into his pale-brown eyes and sighed

as though she were with an inexperienced child. "Don't worry, beloved. It will be fine."

He frowned and let his hands stray to hers. He squeezed them and looked earnestly into her own brown eyes. "Deana . . . you must understand that I cannot marry you. My situation . . . my financial situation is such that I cannot marry unless it is into money." He turned from her. "I should not have . . . taken such advantage of you this evening."

She touched his arm, urged him to look at her. "Alistair . . . I love you. I came to you . . . wanted you. . . ."

He sighed and led her to the door. "This can get us nowhere, Deana. I . . . I am sorry." He opened his door, but she stood at its threshold.

Brandy heard the creak of the door and dived behind an armoire and snuffed out her candle-light. She could hear Deana's voice, soft, husky, and full with affection. She could hear Alistair, impatient, worried, anxious to be done. What was this? Alistair and Deana?

Deana's arms wound themselves around his neck, and on tiptoe she went up for his kiss. He tried to resist her, for he knew this could only lead to trouble.

She put up a brow. "Why, Alistair . . . so cold . . . when only moments ago . . ."

"Hush, Deana. Can't you see I am trying to spare you? You must forget about tonight. It was wrong."

"I see. You are trying to shield me. Well, I tell

122

you openly, Alistair . . . you shan't have to. I don't mean to stand by and watch you wed Lara!" Her voice, though a whisper, was harsh, almost grating.

"That is not something you can prevent."

"Isn't it, though?" she said defiantly.

"At any rate, I haven't decided to marry Lara," he said before he realized what effect it would have.

"Oh?" Her eyes narrowed. "I see what it is. 'Tis her friend . . . that Fernwood chit!"

"If she will have me," he said quietly. "Now, Deana . . . I have been honest with you . . . go back to your room. Forget about me."

"Alistair, mark me well. You will end with no one for wife if you don't choose me."

He shook her. "Stop it! You are allowing your emotions to run away with your good sense." He set her away and ran a hand through his hair. "Dash it, girl . . . if I were able . . . perhaps . . . perhaps you and I . . . but I am not . . . and things have not gone as well . . . as I had hoped. . . . *Now go to bed!*" With this he closed the door and left her standing in the dark.

Brandy heard her walk off to her own quarters and breathed a sigh of relief. Things were certainly proving to be hectic this night. It was amazing what one could learn walking the halls of the Abbey after midnight!

Morning brought a drizzle of rain. Gray skies and darker clouds gave an eerie halo to the earth. Gold and russet leaves were washed to the ground, and chestnuts fell in profusion. Brandy dressed in contrast to the day, donning a bright morning gown of aqua blue. It was well fitted to her form, and its high collar and long sleeves protected her from the damp chill in the halls.

She breakfasted with Denny alone in the conservatory, where the scent of peaches from the dwarf peach trees filled the air. Everyone seemed to be sequestered to their rooms for the morning. Brandy was thoughtful and quiet, and Denny soon found her dull company. He had to repeat to her twice his intention of going out.

"What? Out? Oh no, my friend. You have studies you must attend to if you are going to return to Eton next month," she answered finally. "Now up with you, or must I send you to the vicar to get you to work?"

"You are hard on me, Brandy. Remember I'm a sick boy," he answered with an engaging smile. "I only wanted to go to the stables and see how Lara's mare is doing. She should be getting ready to drop her foal soon."

"Lara's mare has a good three weeks to go. I checked on her yesterday, and well you know it. You want to hobnob with those stable boys, so don't try to hoax me and we shall deal well enough."

"Aw . . . Brandy . . . I only wanted to find out if they knew when the next Rat Pit Event was due."

"Rat Pit?" She wrinkled her nose. Cockfights were bad enough, but she simply in no way could understand the fascination for this particular sport. "I tell you what, Denny. If you finish the studies

I've laid out for you, and *if* the rain subsides, you may accompany me into town this afternoon."

He threw his arms around her neck. "You are a great gun, Brandy!" With this he hurried out of the room and left Brandy to stir her coffee and ponder what next she would do.

Without waiting to finish her coffee, she got to her feet and made purposefully towards the central hall, up the stairs, and to Lara's bedroom. She might be overstepping, she might be considered an interfering, overbearing, prying friend, but she was a friend, and as such she was not going to stand by and watch Lara hide her head and forget her duties!

She knocked soundly and waited. No answer. Within Lara hoped whoever it was would go away. Brandy knocked again and tried the knob. The door was locked.

"Lara!" she said firmly. "Open this door."

Lara blinked. Something in Brandy's tone moved her, and she rose from her window seat, came to the door, opened it a crack, and said wearily, "Y-es?"

"By Jupiter!" exclaimed Brandy, pushing her way within. "Look at you!" Indeed the girl looked white, her hair unkempt and her spirit listless. "I'd wager a monkey you have not been eating!"

"I have not been hungry," said Lara, moving away.

Brandy closed the door and forced Lara around. "Dash it, Lara, I am ashamed of you!"

"What . . . what do you mean?"

"Don't you care about Denny?" There was no

125

sense trying to make Lara pick up herself on her own account. Denny would have to serve as a tool here.

"Denny? Is he unwell again?" Lara's eyes grew frightened.

"If he were, I could blame it on you!" said Brandy harshly.

"What . . . what do you mean?" repeated Lara dully. "I . . . 'tis not my fault he suffers from consumption."

Brandy stamped her foot. "Denny is recovering totally. He does not suffer from consumption. When I asked you to trust me, to leave him to my care, you were good enough to do just that. However I did not then realize you would hold yourself up here alone and neglect the boy!"

"Neglect him? I do not . . . but . . ."

"Lara." Brandy pulled her along to a chair and forced her into it. "Sit." She sighed. "Now, perhaps you will listen to me and understand. Do you remember Caroline? You must."

"Caroline . . . yes . . . there was a scandal about her death. . . ."

"Arsenic poisoning. She had been using it in her powders and creams and even taking a dose of it now and then. She didn't realize that her failing health was caused by it."

"What . . . what has that . . ."

"If Denny were to . . . Lara, who inherits? You?"

"I . . . I am his guardian . . . and . . . Papa has left me a comfortable but not enormous portion," she said with a frown.

"Who comes into the title . . . into the Quendon fortune?"

"Why . . . Alistair is next in line."

Brandy found rushing air passing through her lungs. So, Alistair inherited from Denny. Alistair, who was now acting as agent for the estate.

"Lara, someone has been trying to poison Denny," said Brandy quietly.

"No . . . no . . ." cried Lara.

"He has eaten only what I have seen to these days, and let me tell you, never before have I spent so much time in the kitchens!"

"But . . . at Marden's last night . . ."

"He ate from the carving board, from the main servers. I gave him my glass of lemonade, took his own. No, I have not allowed anything to pass to him without my being sure of its contents. And Lara, he is better, so much better."

"What are you saying? Someone in *my* home is trying to kill my brother?" It was a whisper.

"Yes. Last night we were attacked by highwaymen."

"Oh mercy . . . you were unharmed?" cried Lara, scarcely able to comprehend what she was being told.

"Yes. Marden came just in time . . . and I had my gun . . . but never mind. Lara . . . I am convinced they were after Denny, not jewels."

"Why?"

"The poisoning—slow poisoning so that no one would become suspicious—did not work. Our blackguard had to resort to other means."

"What . . . what shall I do? Brandy, what shall I

127

do? Send Denny away. We must send him away . . . where he will be safe."

"Do not think of it, Lara. We must discover who it is that wants to do away with him or Denny will not be safe anywhere."

"Alistair. It must be . . . he inherits."

Brandy became thoughtful. "How to prove it if it is so, is quite another thing. We must find a way of trapping whoever it is behind this."

"With my brother as bait? No, Brandy . . . 'tis too dangerous."

"Precisely why I wanted Reg or Marden to lend me his aid, but they won't believe me." She shook her head. "I shall have to think on it."

"Marden? You told Marden?" Lara's back was up.

"Why . . . yes. He did rescue us last night."

"Perhaps he planned it. Perhaps he rescued you to throw suspicion away from himself."

"Don't be nonsensical. Denny loves him . . . and why would Marden want Denny out of the way?"

"To get those southwest lands that run along his property. He wants them for the water."

"How would getting rid of Denny enable him to get those lands?"

"I don't know. . . . Maybe . . . he and Alistair are friendly . . . maybe Alistair has offered to sell them to him."

"Why wouldn't Denny?"

"Papa asked Denny to hold onto them always."

"Lara . . . why don't you like Marden?"

Lara moved uncomfortably. "I have my reasons

... but more important, Brandy ... he has his reasons to despise me ... and Denny."

"You cannot be right. He loves Denny."

"Does he? Sometimes I wonder if it is all an act. I tell you, Brandy, he has good cause to hate us."

Brandy frowned. "What is that reason?"

"I ... I cannot tell you," said Lara, looking away.

"All right, then, let us talk about something that touches my family."

"Don't, Brandy. It is useless."

"You love my cousin. I know that you do," said Brandy quietly.

"That is why I must never see him again. Sir Reginald is so very good ... he deserves much more than an alliance with me can give him."

"You are not making any sense. What do you mean?"

"Sir Reginald comes from a good family—"

"So do you!" cut in Brandy. "What has that to say to anything?"

"Brandy ... there is something about me that you don't know. Something terrible. It could come out one day ... and I don't want it to hurt Sir Reginald."

"I don't understand."

"Reggie has political ambitions, and if he were to marry me ... he could be so terribly thwarted in those ambitions. It would be bound to come out, and then Denny would be hurt. This way ... if I don't marry a prominent person, my skeleton will stay hidden."

"I don't believe in that. The dustier a skeleton

the more hideous it becomes, and sooner or later it is uncovered. Better that it be aired when it's clean and easier to face," answered Brandy.

Lara touched her hand, "Do not press me, Brandy. . . ."

"Think about it, Lara . . . and if you are still in the same frame of mind, then at least tell Reg just what your skeleton is. Tell him and allow him the honor of your trust if not your hand."

TWELVE

The clouds had lost some of their foreboding, though they still scurried across the sky. There was a glimmer of sun attempting to break through the gray, and the rain had ceased.

Denny lost no time in pointing out these facts to Brandy and took her by the hand to drag her into the hall and have her step outside to see for herself.

"But Denny . . . wait until I've fetched my redingote at least," she said and laughed amiably.

The front door opened wide before Jeffreys had reached it, and in walked Alistair Hayward. He stood in his top hat over his light-brown curls, his single-tiered dark greatcoat, his top boots somewhat muddied, and Brandy found it difficult to think of this man with his weathered mien as a ruthless murderer. Yet it was a possibility.

131

He saw Denny and ruffled the boy's hair, which immediately brought a scowl to Denny's face. This was a thing allowed only to the lad's favorites, and though Denny tolerated his cousin, he had no great love for the man. "We were just going out," said Denny to Alistair.

Alistair smiled at Brandy and took up her hand to lightly brush it against his lips. He came up from his bow and said in a low voice, "You are as always, Miss Fernwood, breathtaking."

"If, sir, you are short of breath, I would attribute it to all your gadding about," she said lightly. "You are a busy man."

He looked at her thoughtfully a moment. "Denny says you are off? I would suggest that both of you dress warmly." His tone was genuinely concerned.

"So I have been trying to tell him." She turned to Denny. "Why don't you go up and fetch both our coats, pumpkin?"

Readily Denny agreed and took the stairs in a hurry. Once again Alistair reclaimed Brandy's attention.

"Where are you off to?"

"I thought I would do some shopping in town."

"Then I am in luck. I have to go into town myself to see Denny's solicitors. I've only stopped by to pick up those papers I worked on last night." He gazed at her warmly. "I shall be pleased to take you in my carriage, if you wouldn't mind my company."

"Thank you, Mr. Hayward. That would be very nice," she answered demurely. She wanted to know more about the man.

His voice lowered. "I missed you at dinner last evening."

"Oh, were you here for dinner? How nice for your mother and Deana, for I am told Lara took her meal in her room."

He sighed. "Yes, but I am afraid I wasn't much company for them. I worked late into the night on the ledger sheets and then went up to the blue room my mother always keeps in readiness for me here."

"You didn't stay at your cottage, then?" She knew full well he had not.

"No, though I did go there early this morning." He started to move off, for Denny had reappeared, "Well, I'll just get those papers and we can be off."

Marden put a hand to his tight mouth. His black hair fell in waves to his neckline. His aqua-blue eyes were dark in thought. There was nothing more to hold him at the Towers. Fisk was right, they should be in London, enjoying all its frivolities and its women. In his mind was a copper-haired woman whose green eyes teased joy into his reluctant heart. On his lips burned the memory of her kiss. It was she who kept him here. And there was Denny.

Sir Reginald had confided Brandy's fears to Lord Marden and hence was able to laugh them off. Marden had listened and marveled that the girl had come to much the same opinion he had himself. What to do? A difficult dilemma here. He was in no position to do very much. Lara did not trust him. He did not trust all the rest.

"Dash it, Kurt . . . we could be packed and off tomorrow," complained Fisk. "There ain't even a promise of a cockfight to keep us."

"What of Miss Fernwood? Do you think she would allow us to take her off in such haste?" returned Marden.

"Must, you know. There it is, but can't stay without Reg . . . and Reg there can't get away fast enough."

Sir Reginald stood by the park window absently gazing on Marden lands. Brandy had told him nothing about Lara last night. Lara had refused to see her. There was no reason why he should stay on, and yet he was finding it hard to leave. He said nothing to Fisk's remark.

"What you need, Fisk, is some diversion. Come on, we will go into town and see what we can get up in the way of sport," offered Marden merrily enough. He wasn't about to leave for London just yet. Not with Denny's fate on the precarious edge of uncertainty. Nor would he leave the problem to Brandy alone, and he knew that she would not return to London now.

"Do you join us, Reg?"

"What? No . . . I think I shall laze about with a book."

"Blue-deviled," said Fisk in what he thought was a whisper.

Hayward tooled his single horse, and gave over a dialogue of interesting information to Brandy, who sat wedged between him and Denny in the open curricle.

134

She adjusted the blanket he had set over her knees and made certain that Denny's twisting had not dislodged the cover from his lap.

The approach to the quiet little market village of Wotton-Under-Edge was something of a climb, as the village was set on a tuft of high ground.

"The village got its real start with the wool trade in the seventeenth century," put in Hayward informatively as Brandy remarked upon its loveliness.

Tiled roofs gleamed red, quaint old names tickled the imagination, such as Ludgate Hill and the Chipping, which housed the original market square. An impressive fourteenth-century church loomed before them, and Brandy exclaimed excitedly that she would love to explore it.

"Its naught but a church!" ejaculated Denny in some disgust.

"But an old one, Denny. Only think . . . it has survived the forces of weather and man and is still in use. Wouldn't you like to have a look?"

"Don't need to. Been here often enough, and besides, the vicar might be about."

She laughed. "What are you worried about, Denny?"

"Might want to read me a lecture," suggested Denny dourly. "Best I stay in the carriage."

"Very well then, young lord," returned Hayward, anxious enough to be alone with Brandy. "Here are the reins. Keep old Blue standing—we won't be above five minutes or so." He jumped down from the curricle and turned to catch up Brandy in his firm grasp.

He put her down, but his fingers still held her small trim waist lingeringly. "They have an organ within. Its case is an exceptionally handsome piece with something of a history."

"Splendid," she answered excitedly but pulled herself out of his hold. "I have a penchant for history." She led him down the flagstone path to the high-arched entrance.

The high-domed nave echoed their footsteps as he led her past stained-glass windows, stone carvings, and statues towards the organ that dominated a good portion of one wall. She found the old gothic church awesome but beckoning, elaborate in its artifacts and yet basic in its form. It did what churches of its time attempted to do—give their worshipers a vision of heaven.

The wooden case of the organ was intricately carved and solidly built. Brandy crooned over its commanding attention, and Alistair smiled, well pleased to tell her something of its past.

"This came originally from St. Martin's-in-the-Fields in London, where it had been residing as a gift from George I. In 1799 St. Martin's was undergoing some renovation and it was offered up for sale. Our vicar managed to purchase it for two hundred guineas."

"A good price," exclaimed Brandy.

"Indeed, when one considers that its original cost was near to sixteen hundred guineas!" agreed Alistair. "Come . . . shall I show you more of its past?" He seemed to be taking her to the back of the church, and she thought immediately of Denny alone.

"No, you have business in town . . . and I have already taken advantage of your time."

"You could never take advantage, Miss Fernwood. My time is your own."

"You are very gallant, but Denny does await us. . . ."

He inclined his head and allowed her to turn. However, as they reached the arched open entrance through which they had come, Brandy caught the heel of her half-boot on a jagged idle stone and tripped. Alistair caught her neatly in his arms and unbent in order to pull her up.

Marden saw Denny fiddling with the ribbons as the boy sat in the curricle, and his brow went up. He slowed his dapple gray to a walk and looked about for Brandy.

"It's about time we did some walking. Damn if you didn't work me this ride," complained Fisk.

"It was just what you needed, old boy!" However, the smile froze on his face when his searching eyes discovered the object of his inquiry neatly in the arms of Alistair Hayward. His lips tightened as he took in the arresting vision, and he felt a swell of unfamiliar emotions rattle his temper.

"I say," announced Fisk, looking across a moment later to find Brandy leading Alistair back to the waiting curricle and Denny, "here is Brandy!" He made an admiring click between his teeth. "Damn if she isn't the finest-looking female ever I have come across. Knows how to dress, too. Not all of 'em do, you know, but Brandy has the trick of it."

Marden's eyes ran over Brandy in her aqua twilled silk redingote. It suited both her fair complexion and her copper curls. Its lines were basic and neatly fitted at the bodice and waist. Her aqua matching silk bonnet sat fetchingly upon her bright curls, and there was no denying that she quite attracted a man's second glance.

He tipped his curly-brimmed top hat to her, and his aqua eyes raked her disapprovingly. He would have her know that he had seen her in Alistair's arms. "Miss Fernwood? Enjoying our church?"

She bristled. She was fully aware that he had seen and misunderstood her mishap in the doorway of the church. How dare he think she was in the habit of . . . no doubt she had not taken stern enough revenge on him last night! Well, she would show him she did not care one dot for his opinion. Why should she?

"Oh yes, my lord. Mr. Hayward was kind enough to give me a tour of the building."

"Are you going into town, Brandy?" asked Fisk hopefully. "Shall we join you?"

She hesitated. She had no wish to hurt Fisk, but she didn't want his arrogant companion to think that she welcomed his company as well.

"Mr. Hayward was kind enough to take us up, for I mean to do some shopping while he attends to his business."

"Famous," cried Fisk. "We can all go over to that little sweetshop for tea and cake after you finish your shopping. Denny will like that, won't you, lad?"

"Aye . . . but don't tell me you want to go looking

138

at ribbons, sir?" asked Denny conspiratorily of Fisk.

Fisk knew when something was in the wind. He leaned towards the lad. "Never had any such notion in mind. Why?"

"Hear tell that a . . ." Denny lowered his voice, hoping Brandy would not hear. "There is a . . . rat pit been set up. . . ."

"By Jove, lad, are you sure?" asked Fisk in some excitement. "Haven't been to one of those since . . . never mind. It's been a long time. Where shall we inquire about it?"

Alistair had started his horse forward by this time, and the curricle moved onto the road. Fisk rode beside Denny; Marden kept his horse and his thoughts in check just behind Fisk.

"Thought while Brandy was busy I would lope off to the Red Lion Inn. The lads there will be knowing for sure," said Denny.

Brandy sighed. "Denny . . . I don't know if I want you going to such a thing. . . ."

"I'm a lord, girl. I can go if I want," he said on a cocky note.

"You are a lord, there is no denying that, and I am just the sort of female who has always wanted to take a stick to the bottom of one!" returned Brandy.

"Aw go on, you wouldn't," he dared.

"If you ever talk to me or any other in such a tone, I very well can and will, my lord Quendon."

He grinned sheepishly. "Only doing the part up brown. It's good practice."

She had started to tweak his nose when Fisk

139

once again called her attention. "At least let the lad come with us to look into the matter. Marden here will look after him." While his consideration for the child's amusement moved him to speak on Denny's behalf, it did not move him so far as to offer to be the boy's chaperon.

Marden eyed his friend quizzically, but agreed. "Do allow him to join the two of us, Miss Fernwood. I fancy he will be the better for some male companionship."

"Oh!" snapped the lady, taking instant umbrage.

Marden momentarily wondered why he who always made the females swoon with his wit and charm seemed forever to be offending this one.

They had pulled up beside the town hostelry, where they would leave their horses during their stay in town, and Hayward was jumping down from his seat, putting the reins into the livery boy's hands, and turning to help Miss Fernwood alight.

In some annoyance he saw her follow Denny, who scampered past Marden's hands, which in turn found Brandy's trim waist. Slowly, audaciously, he lowered her to the ground, and his eyes glinted as they met her pools of green.

"The ribbon shop is just across the village green, Miss Fernwood. Shall I escort you there?"

"No, I think not. Thank you, Mr. Hayward," said Brandy, allowing him to take up her gloved hand.

"Then I shall see you again . . . in two hours' time, shall we say?"

"Thank you, that will be lovely."

"At the sweet shop," put in Fisk.

A moment later Alistair had left them and Denny was again tugging on Brandy's sleeve.

"If you want me to guard you around town, Brandy . . . I will be honored to do it," said the lad, bravely putting his desires aside, for it occurred to him that this might be why she did not want him running off with Fisk and Marden.

This did her in, of course. "Nonsense. You go ahead with Marden and Fisk and discover where that dreadful rat pit is to be held."

"You are a grand old girl!" cried the boy, and then, taking up Fisk's hand, he began pulling the man along.

Marden stopped. "Depend upon it, Miss Fernwood, he shall come to no harm while in my company." With that he turned, and with a half-frown she watched the three jauntily move off.

THIRTEEN

Happily Brandy browsed through swags of bright ribbons and trimmings, fingered various rolls of material, contemplating the style of gown she could put them to. After some twenty minutes she had made a selection and brought her choices to the counter, where a buxom middle-aged woman beneath a prim white cap and starched apron pleasantly waited on her.

The jingle of the bell announced another customer, and Brandy looked up to find Rose, the pretty little gypsy girl, padding softly into the shop. The girl's hair had been pulled into a bun at the back of her neck, and a dark wool shawl covered her shoulders. She looked a trifle wary, but a length of ivory silk caught her eye and with a soft sound of admiration she moved towards it.

Brandy was smiling to herself when suddenly

the smile was whipped off her face. The buxom, pleasant shopwoman changed into a raging thing of cruelty as she swept down on the gypsy girl and took her by the arm.

"Ye get out of 'ere!"

"But I . . ." Rose held up a purse. "I came to buy some—"

"Not in my shop ye don't buy! Ye want somethin' ye go down to Old Ned's place. Maybe he'll take yer money. I won't."

Rose hung her head. "He does not have what I want. . . ." She started to turn and go out.

"Just a minute!" said Brandy on a note of horror. "Why in heaven's name are you doing this?" She wondered if perhaps the girl and this woman had ever had any trouble.

"*She's a gypsy!* Thieving bunch of sinners! I don't serve 'em," said the woman, folding her hands in front of her.

"I am not a thief!" cried Rose. "I have money with which to buy what I want."

"Ye be the one that dances at that carnival."

"There is no sin in dancing!" put in Brandy. She had moved to stand beside Rose, and no one heard the door jingle and close at their backs.

"Lookee 'ere, miss . . . I got to tell ye that I don't deal with gypsies."

"Don't you? Well then, you'll deal with me." She turned to the girl. "Rose, isn't it?" She had heard her so called the night of the carnival. The girl nodded; her eyes were still downcast. "What is it you wished to purchase?"

"Some finery . . . for my wedding. . . ."

143

"Pick it out and bring it to the counter," said Brandy firmly.

"Maybe ye didn't understand me when I told ye, miss . . . I don't—"

"The thing is that I did understand you, more is the pity. Are you now going to tell me that you won't deal with me either?"

There was a challenge in her eyes, and the shopwoman did not mistake it. She didn't know who this girl was, but that she was quality was evident, and she didn't want trouble with the quality. They could put her out of business.

Lord Marden had come in during this exchange and with his arms folded across his chest leaned into the wall to watch its outcome. He was amused, he was intrigued, he was surprised. Ladies just did not put themselves out for gypsies, but then Miss Fernwood, he had soon learned, was no ordinary lady!

If this was a daughter of nobility, thought the shopwoman, there was no saying what they could do. She had heard tales of how certain dukes and such put poor women like her out of business for nothing more than an imagined insult. She held her tongue as Rose collected the items she wanted and put them on the counter.

Out of their sight, but enjoying the scene, stood Lord Marden, with his hands folded over his chest, his hat rakishly to one side over one brow. Would Miss Fernwood never cease to amaze him? She was a gently nurtured, quality-bred daughter of blood. A lady. Did she not realize that ladies did not go about the countryside brandishing guns, making accusations of foul play, and defending gypsies? It was unheard of. Ladies were soft and magical beings meant to please a man. It occurred to him that the soft and magical beings he had hitherto encountered had never served to please half as much as Miss Fernwood did for half as long. Odd that, but never mind, she was a lively piece that would surely drive hard any man she chose to have.

Gruffly the shopwoman gave Miss Fernwood the total. Brandy slid the money she withdrew from her own reticule across the counter, took up the packages, and smiled to the girl. "Come now, we are done here."

"But . . . I must pay you. . . ."

"So you must, for I am honored to deal with you," returned Brandy, accepting the exact sum she had laid out and putting it away. At that she turned to find Marden coming towards her.

"My lord," she said in some surprise as he took up her arm and tipped his hat to the pretty gypsy.

Rose dropped a quick curtsy, thanked Miss Fernwood again, and hurried away. Marden had looked nice enough, but lords such as himself could be dangerous to dark-eyed young gypsy girls. It had been drummed into her head, and she was taking no chances.

Brandy frowned as she watched the girl scramble out of sight. "It isn't right." She sighed.

"No, it isn't," he agreed. "And I see you are the sort who pays more than lip service to her beliefs." His aqua eyes were admiring, and he was amused to see her flush.

"What are you doing here?" she said to change the subject as he started her across the road.

"Fisk and Denny are in the sweetshop securing for us a private table where we might be comfortable."

"And did Denny's inquiries discover the whereabouts of the rat pit?" She was smiling.

"It did, and I am afraid you will be met with what you may find hideous descriptions of the sport he means to badger you into allowing him to attend."

"Drat," said the lady.

He laughed shortly, and then, on another note, "He is very charming. I am not surprised that you find him . . . captivating."

"Who?" she asked in some surprise.

"Alistair Hayward," he answered dryly. "And though he no doubt finds your meager fortune attractive, I rather think he is not blind to your undeniable beauty."

She wanted to slap him, but the truth of his words touched her indeflatable honesty.

"I rather think, my lord, that 'tis my fortune that moves him. In fact, I think he vacillates between Lara and myself. True though it is that neither of us is fat, hoary, and haggish, it is not our winsome personalites or ravishing flesh that induces his court. No, while you say *he* is not blind, I must have you know that I too am not blind."

He stopped to look at her, and prevented her from moving away by firmly holding her wrist. "And, piqued, you sought to cut your friend out of

146

the picture. Thus your pretty behavior with him in the church?" There was a sneer to his sensual mouth.

She was enraged by his words. Could he really think such a thing of her? "You may think what you like, for I intend to carry on as I see fit, and you, my lord, are overstepping!"

She moved forward, and he held the sweetshop door open for her. His tone was low, almost savage.

"If, sweetheart, you believe I am overstepping, then I must disagree with you and say, yea, you are blind!" His eyes glinted dangerously.

It was fortunate that Brandy chose to ignore his remark and sweep past him towards Fisk and Denny, who rose quickly at her entrance. Had she chosen to demand that he explain himself, he would have been hard put to do so!

Some moments later Brandy was fiercely spreading butter on her slice of bread, and glaring at his lordship as she bit into the thing. He sipped his tea, considered her thoughtfully and gave her stare for glare until she turned away in some confusion. There had been a look in his aqua eyes that was most disconcerting.

"It is this afternoon, Brandy, just outside of town—they have constructed a six-foot round pit just for today's event."

"That seems very costly just for one event?" remarked Brandy in spite of herself.

"I think they have built its walls out of wood instead of the polished cement they use in the city," returned Lord Marden.

147

"Yes, well, that is all very interesting, but I do not think that Denny should—"

"Have you ever seen a ratting event, Brandy?" glowed Denny as he hurried to interrupt her. He had hit home, and he knew it, for Fisk had told him that Sir Reginald had taken her to one or two when she had been a rough-and-tumble youth. He knew his mark well.

She blushed. "As a matter of fact . . . I have been, but—"

"And you would deny it to me?"

"But . . . Alistair comes for us soon," she put in lamely.

"We can hire horses for the trip home," put in Marden quietly.

"Horses?" she asked, her brow up.

"Unless of course you wish to make the trip back with Mr. Hayward alone?" said Marden dryly.

"I wish to remain with Denny," she shot at him on a hot note. "In spite of the . . . circumstances." She blighted him with her icy look.

"Denny," she tried again, "are you sure you want to see such a thing?"

He nodded vigorously, and she sighed. "Very well . . . but here is your cousin, come to fetch us. . . ."

Denny spread some of his clotted cream on his scone, dropped a spoonful of jam on top of this, and proceeded to fill his mouth. Fisk observed the lad with some appreciation and followed suit. It was left to Marden and Brandy to explain.

"Mr. Hayward," said Brandy, smiling, "I am

afraid that we are still enjoying our tea. Won't you join us?"

"I think not, but please do not rush." He drew up a chair.

"Young Quendon here has convinced Brandy to allow him to see the rat pit event being held on the outskirts of town. Do you have to get back, or can you join us?" said Marden lightly.

Alistair looked surprised and smiled ruefully. "I am afraid I am committed to my books this afternoon." He turned to Brandy. "I am sure the rat pit holds no lure for you, though, Miss Fernwood. I shall be happy to see you home before I lope off to my cottage."

"That will be out of your way, sir, and there is no need. I think I shall keep Denny in hand."

"But how will you return?" He was a little irritated.

"Marden says he can hire horses for us." She touched his arm, "But thank you . . . Alistair." She was being kind.

Alistair felt himself ahead in the game and touched the gloved hand at his arm. *"You* never have to thank me for anything." He rose and bent over her hand. "Your very obedient servant, Miss Fernwood." He parted from the assembled group, and Brandy turned to find Marden's eyes blistering!

The admission charge was only one penny. Next to the half crown that was charged for cockfighting, it was inexpensive. Therefore the crowd it drew came from the lower classes—gambling men, cits, laborers out of work and heady for sport, and the few women present were not the sort that Marden wished around Brandy. She might have attended such a thing with Sir Reginald when they were children, but this was no place for her now. More than likely some chap foxed out of his mind might see fit to take a liberty with her and thus embroil them all in rather more sport than they presently wanted.

He turned to Fisk. "See to it that Denny enjoys himself this evening. Take him to dinner afterwards and then see him home to Quendon Abbey."

"Why should you be the one to take Brandy home?" objected Fisk.

"Because you are the one who has a hundred little gold ones on that mongrel you picked out earlier." Marden laughed.

Fisk's eyes widened. "So I do. Right, then . . . for this is no place for our girl, is it?"

"You know that it's not. I shall leave the horses with you, but Fisk, you ride my gray, and go easy on his mouth or he will run you into a tree!"

"I am not ham-handed you know," returned Fisk, taking umbrage.

"No, but he is sweet-mouthed." With this he turned and moved to take up Brandy's arm.

Brandy had been frowning as they approached the crowd pressing in towards the six-foot round pit. She could see the men already vying for the best seats around the deep trench. She could hear the dogs barking, and a sudden feeling of weakness hit her stomach. She really didn't want to watch those poor dogs attack and kill a pack of rats. She really didn't want to be a part of such a thing. As a young girl, much of it had been exciting because it had been the forbidden. But she remembered now the blood . . . the viciousness . . . the wagers . . . no. She looked around her with a dubious expression as the boisterous humor of some of the rougher individuals became quite scandalous. However, suddenly Marden was pulling her away, taking her out of their sight.

"Come along quickly now. You are not going there!"

She had no liking for his imperious attitude. "I shall go where I please!" she announced on a stubborn note.

At that moment a large man with a week's growth of whiskers and the smell of gin took into his arms the plump maid he had just met some moments ago in an obscure corner of town. Heartily he embraced the woman, and they fell limply against the walls of the gray weathered wood of an outhouse. Brandy's eyes grew wider still, for they were not ten feet away, and clearly she could see the man become amorously familiar with his female companion.

Marden observed this and said sardonically, "Well, of course, Miss Fernwood, I did not realize this is what pleased you."

Brandy blushed hotly and stomped off towards town once more, leaving the rat pit behind her. With something of a devilish grin, Marden followed and fell into step beside her. He said thoughtfully, hoping to return her attention more favorably on himself, "I thought I would hire a small curricle and take you . . . home, if the idea meets with your approbation."

She eyed him warily, for the hesitation on the word "home" was not lost on her. "To whose home, my lord?"

"Why, to mine, of course," he answered glibly and pushed open the carriage house's door for her to pass through.

FOURTEEN

Diverted by the hostelry attendant, Marden was not able to give Miss Fernwood his undivided attention. As she was not willing to settle for less than this, she refrained from retorting, saving it, as it were, until they could be alone and she would be free to tell his lordship exactly what she thought of his proposal.

However, some minutes elapsed, during which time Brandy's quicksilver temper dropped its feverish pitch and she began to reflect on the evening to come. Go to his home indeed! But the alternative was an evening at Quendon Abbey. A dinner with Cynthia Hayward and Deana Hopkins. Lara would no doubt take dinner in her own quarters again, which was just as well, as Brandy found herself out of patience with the girl's behavior. Hayward had gone to his cottage, and Denny was with Fisk. She sighed heavily. She had by that time been seated beside Lord Marden, who tooled the curricle's single horse down the main road out of the village.

He heard her sigh and mistook its meaning. He looked long at her and said in a level voice, "If joining your cousin and myself for dinner so distresses you, Miss Fernwood, I shall take you up to the Abbey."

She glanced around sharply and discovered his profile had for an infinitesimal space in time taken on the look of a stricken boy. For no reason at all she found herself touched. Her resolve reeled. "Will not the proprieties be offended, my lord?" she offered doubtfully.

"Proprieties indeed! Sir Reginald, I need not remind you, is your cousin, which is chaperon itself. He did travel the distance with you and Fisk from London, did he not?" He did not wait for her answer. "And forgetting that, there is my housekeeper, who serves the purpose well enough."

Brandy laughed. "Yes, I could not help but notice her the other night as she sidled in and out of sight. She is a veritable dragon, my lord, if you will forgive me for saying so."

"Then it is settled?" He beamed as though he were indeed a boy just given a much-sought-after prize.

His expression totally disarmed Brandy, and she found herself relaxing to his easy conversation, laughing to his many hilarious anecdotes, and smiling at some of his philosophies. There was much substance to this Lord Rake she had not hitherto suspected.

The sun still had not forced its might through the swiftly racing clouds. The new day had not dispersed the damp air, but Brandy was grateful that at least it was not raining. She urged her horse into a canter, paced her well, and took the log flying. She had taken the wrong turn a few moments ago and was backtracking. No one knew what she was about this morning, for she had not trusted anyone, not even Lara, who was acting so very peculiar.

Denny had promised to stay in his schoolroom and attack his books, and so she had donned her emerald-green riding habit, set her matching velvet top hat atop her copper curls, and gone to the stables, where discreetly she inquired after Dr. Franklin's residence. She meant to question the good doctor and determine for herself what next she should do.

Dr. Franklin removed his spectacles, laid them on the desk before him, and rose to his feet as Marden was shown into the study by the doctor's housekeeper.

"My lord, won't you sit down and join me for a cup of tea?" said the doctor pleasantly.

Lord Marden remained standing and gazed gravely at the older man. "I think not, sir."

"Oh?" The doctor frowned in puzzlement. "Is something . . . wrong?"

"Why don't you tell me?" said Marden, moving

about the room easily and turning on his last word to look askance at the doctor.

"I . . . I don't know what you mean."

"Don't you? Perhaps it would help if I told you we are speaking of young Lord Quendon." Marden's voice was low and ominous.

Dr. Franklin felt a flood of heat swell his neck. His finger played at his collar. "I . . . I have not been called up to the house. Has something gone wrong there?"

"Something has gone wrong, but Miss Fernwood has managed to set it right."

"I don't understand. . . ." Perspiration began to glitter on the doctor's forehead.

Marden was aware of the signs, and his brow went up. "Don't you, doctor? Consumption was the diagnosis, I think, wasn't it, Franklin?"

"Young Quendon . . . are you telling me he has taken a turn for the better?" inquired the doctor, attempting to regain his composure. Think, think, what to do?

"That is precisely what I am telling you. Didn't you think he would?" Marden shook his head. "No, of course you did not, you were given to believe the lad might soon die. Why did you think that, Franklin?" Marden was moving dangerously forward.

Franklin took a step backwards. "My examination . . . the lad was suffering . . . I might have made a mistake . . ."

"You made a mistake, doctor," said Marden carefully. "Don't make another where young Quendon is concerned." He picked up his hat and gloves from the table and turned his back to leave Franklin in serious conjecture.

Finally Brandy could see the doctor's cottage across a neatly trimmed lawn, and then her eyes opened wide at the unmistakable figure of Lord Marden mounting his dapple gray. He wore a buckskin riding coat and breeches. His beaver top hat was pulled low over one eye, and he took to horse nimbly. She watched him ride down the drive and turn off at the main road. What had he been doing at Franklin's? Her brows puckered over her pert nose and she urged her horse forward.

A few moments later Dr. Franklin was once again greeting another visitor in his study. This time he moved away from his fire, where he had been delving into his karma. A small tired smile met Brandy as she came forward and gave her gloved hand to him.

He touched it lightly and led her to a comfortable lady's chair near the hearth.

"Now, Miss Fernwood, how may I help you?"

"Perhaps, doctor, this time *I* might be able to help *you*," she said quietly.

He frowned. "What is it you are getting at? I would have plain speaking, if you please."

"Would you? Very well. Denny has been in my care the past five days. . . . Not a drop of arsenic has managed to find its way to his lips." She noted that while he looked frightened, he was not shocked.

He blanched. "Arsenic?"

157

"Yes, doctor. I think upon careful consideration you might find that another examination of Denny might be needed to reassure his sister that the lad is not suffering from consumption."

"My dear young woman—"

"It is only a suggestion. I thought it only fair that you be given an opportunity to consider your own position before another doctor is called in."

He stared at her for a long moment, and clearly defeat was in his eyes. "I see, Miss Fernwood."

She got to her feet. "Then we shall expect you at the Abbey?"

"Of course," he said simply and followed her to the door. He saw her out of his house and turned hurriedly to his housekeeper.

"See that my things are packed. I am going to South Wales on an extended visit to my sister."

The housekeeper's jaw dropped in surprise. "But sir . . . there be Mrs. Angus . . . due to deliver next week . . ."

"She will have to make due with the local midwife, for I shan't be here!" Clearly things had gone out of control. He had risked much while caught up in heady passion for Cynthia Hayward, but no more. He was not going to put his head knowingly into the noose. Marden knew. Now this chit. No, he would take himself carefully out of the picture. In that manner no blame could be placed at his door!

Denny doodled on his writing page. It wasn't fair that he had to stay cooped up when he was feeling so fit. He glanced out his window and

158

noted one of his female setters carrying her pup by the scruff of the neck and smiled. Maybe he would just go out for a bit? Just to play with the puppies for a time. He could always study later. He picked up his wool cap, plopped it on his head, slipped into his shortcoat, and peeped into the hall. No one about. Quietly he slipped down the back stairs and out a side door to freedom.

Not very much later Brandy returned to the house and without bothering to remove her emerald velvet top hat or kid gloves she hurriedly took the stairs in search of Denny. He was not in his room, so she too took the back stairs and sped down the narrow corridor that led past the garden doors of the conservatory. There she heard a sound and stopped, thinking it might be Denny.

"You must be aware, my lord, that at present I have not the power to . . . grant you the sale of the tract of land you so desire." It was Alistair Hayward and his reply denoted to Brandy Marden's obvious question.

She moved closer to the glass wall. She could just make out their forms past the thick green shrubbery within. Why had they retired to such a secluded part of the house? What was Marden doing? First Dr. Franklin . . . now Alistair?

Marden's voice had an odd underlining to its inflection.

"Perhaps, though, it may soon be within your power to do so."

"I don't really understand your meaning, Marden." It was Alistair now who sounded off key and strangely cautious.

"Oh, I think you do. With Denny's state of health so precariously in the balance, you may soon have enough power to deal with my request."

Brandy put a hand to her mouth and felt a sudden sharp pain shoot through her stomach. Marden? What was Marden saying? How could he speak so callously of Denny . . . and why? Marden knew that Denny was better. Why? Oh God . . . not Marden! Not over a piece of land!

Alistair took a short tour of the tiled floor and touched one of the exotic blooms before turning to look into Marden's eyes.

"This comes as something of a . . . surprise, my lord. I have always assumed you . . . rather cared about the lad."

"And I do, Alistair, I do. I only want to know how things may stand in the future," said Marden.

"That is yet to be seen," answered Alistair thoughtfully. "However, I have never seen why that tract of land was held in abeyance. We do not till the land, and as long as you would make use of it better than we . . . I would most certainly decide to sell it to you . . . should the decision ever fall into *my* hands."

Brandy did not have to hear any more. She ran out the back door, now quite frantic to find Denny and hold him safe within her arms. She was going to cry. No. Why should she feel like crying? Marden, Marden . . . what had he done? Had he made a pact with Alistair? Had he encouraged Alistair to do away with Denny? Her world felt strangely unbalanced as she sped across the lawns and into the woods.

Lara! Where was she? Why wasn't she taking more care of Denny? Didn't she care? If Lara was going to marry Alistair, she would then become the mistress of the home she loved. The thought suddenly made Brandy tremble. Lara . . . ? No, it wasn't possible. Yet someone was trying to get rid of Denny. Could all of them be in on it?

She had to get Denny safely tucked beneath her wing. She had to make Reggie understand, believe. She had to do something soon! She toured the woods, called out his name to no avail. As she turned back towards the abbey she could see him near the walls of the Spanish garden at the back of the conservatory. How had she missed him? She smiled in spite of her fears, for he was sitting on the ground near the wall and in his lap were half a dozen puppies all clambering over him.

She went towards him, cutting across the lawn towards the garden toolshed, past it to where Denny reposed happily against the stone wall.

"Denny," she said on an irritated note, "didn't you promise to finish your work? And all I found on your desk was a goodly stack of empty pages."

He grinned sheepishly up at her. Brandy was more than a friend, more than a sister, for though he had an affection for Lara, she had ever been too gentle, too feminine, to understand him. Brandy understood. It would never have entered his head to question her right to chastise and order him about. He had given her that right early in their first meeting three years ago. "Aw . . . Brandy . . . how could I resist these? The gardener must have left the door to the toolshed open, and Sarah's

161

pups were scampering all over the place. I had to help her find 'em, didn't I?" He dimpled at her. "Don't be cross with me, Brandy."

She took his nose as he stood up. "Scamp. Come on, then, let's return them to the shed and be off, shall we?"

Resigned, he agreed with a sigh. They put the last of the puppies away, took the flagstone steps along the high stone wall towards the conservatory garden doors.

A quick scan of that room told Brandy that the two gentlemen who had earlier occupied it were no longer there. Several arches of Spanish design met with the stone wall that flanked the gardens. They passed under these together until Denny skipped up ahead and began producing a ballad he had heard the night before at the rat pit with Fisk.

Brandy smiled to herself and was about to advise him that the ballad was not something he should be singing in her presence when a sound caught her attention.

Just ahead and above was a large cement urn. It reposed on the high wall where it had been for decades, yet something or someone was causing it to move, to grate against the stone, to totter. In another moment Denny would be just beneath it. Brandy took a hasty step forward, moved by instinct. She let out a scream.

Denny turned with surprise and stood frozen as he watched Brandy race at him. A moment later she had pushed him down and out of the way. However, the urn had come crashing down and

162

caught her heavily on the shoulder. She went down with a thud to the ground, and unable to move with the weight of the crushed cement, winded from the force of the blow, she lay there on her stomach for a few moments unable to speak.

"Brandy! Brandy!" Denny screamed her name in agitation as he bent over her. He didn't see where Lord Marden came from, but Brandy had opened her eyes in time to see him round the corner where another arch led to the other side of the wall. The fact quite made her ill. She licked her lips and attempted to find her voice. But Marden was there, throwing the broken pieces of urn aside, gently scooping her up like a babe, cradling her in his arms. His aqua eyes were scanning her face, his expression undeniably one of total concern. "Don't speak, love, don't . . . you've been thoroughly winded. Try and breathe easy . . . that's a lass. . . ." His voice caressed her. He turned to Denny. "Go on, lad . . . get the doors."

Brandy thought of last night at Marden Towers. They had enjoyed a lovely dinner with her cousin. She had been able to tell Reggie that she had spoken with Lara, that perhaps all was not lost to him, and Reggie's mood had picked up. Marden had been a wonderful host, and later he had taken her home. There had even been a moment when she thought he might again try to kiss her, a moment when she wanted him to, but he had not. And now, everything had changed!

He was laying her down on one of the many lounges that were nestled beneath high greens and spreading ferns. He was undoing the pearl buttons of her white lace collar. He was undoing the buttons of her now dirtied emerald-green velvet jacket. He was brushing away the copper curls from her eyes. She managed a half-smile and her first words were, "My hat . . ."

He laughed and sent Denny after it. A frightened look came into her eyes. "No . . . not Denny . . ."

He patted her hand. "He'll be back in a moment."

She took a long breath. Was this the same man that had conspired only twenty, thirty minutes ago with Alistair Hayward? Had she understood what she had heard? Could she be wrong? Oh . . . but there was an aching soreness in her back . . . her shoulder. She reached to touch it, and Marden pulled gently at the jacket's sleeve, "Here, let's have this off you . . . in case there is swelling."

She allowed him to help, studying his face as he worked the jacket off her. "Marden . . . someone moved the urn . . . it tottered just above Denny's head. I . . . shouldn't have screamed . . . for he froze on the spot. It could have . . . killed him."

Clearly Brandy had been shaken by more than her injuries. He attempted to assuage her fears. "Hush now, love." He touched gently at her thin white blouse and looked as though he might be contemplating its removal.

"Just what do you think you are doing?" she demanded, her flagging spirit suddenly returning.

He grinned. "I merely wanted to ascertain the extent of damage your body has suffered."

"Well, never mind." She moved her left arm,

and though the pain brought a frown over her nose she said lightly, "I am sore enough, but not, I think, broken."

He noted that some color had returned to her cheeks, and his aqua eyes regarded her tenderly. "I am convinced it would take a great deal to break you, sweetheart."

"I am not your sweetheart," she snapped testily. "And you are not going to sweep this affair under the rug!"

His hand took her chin and he grinned to see her pout. "Both are points well taken. The first we shall have to see about. The second, I assure you, is not my intention."

"Then pay me some heed, my lord," she cried suddenly, feeling the weight of protecting Denny was a burden she was not capable of carrying. "Someone means to do Denny in . . . is willing to risk a great deal . . . for whoever it is has made an attempt against Denny in the light of day."

"I am afraid that I must agree with you. We are dealing with someone whose desperation has driven them into ruthlessness," said his lordship on a dark frown. "But I would prefer he moved unhampered. If you set up a cry over this incident, he will go more carefully and be all the harder to flush out."

"My God . . . you mean to use Denny as bait!" she breathed.

"That was not my intention," he said gravely.

"But that is what will happen," she threw at him.

"It will happen regardless. I am hoping that if

our would-be murderer moves about freely, he or . . . she may make a mistake. However," he put up a hand to stall her ready tongue—"if we frighten him off . . . he might seek out a more devious means, and then, my love, where will Denny be?"

"No doubt I shall have to stand idly by and allow this villain to stalk Denny?" She was dubious.

"May I point out to you that you have not been standing idly by?" He kissed the hand he had been holding all the while.

She withdrew it from his touch.

"My lord . . ." She was very near to tears. She didn't know what to think, what to do, and she could still remember hearing Marden and Alistair coldly talking of a future without Denny as master of Quendon Abbey.

"Shall I take Denny back with me to Marden Towers?" he asked.

She looked at him sharply. Many thoughts raced through her mind, and there was no time to eliminate them with logic. Her answer came swiftly, and there was no mistaking her reason.

"No!"

His brows went up. "Oh, I see. I too am suspect." There was a hurt in the recesses of his aqua eyes.

She could see that, and it didn't make sense. It didn't balance with the things he had just said to Alistair Hayward. But then nothing made any sense any more. She blurted it out before she could stop herself.

"There are lands he is unwilling to sell you because of a promise made to his father. Alistair,

166

though, would no doubt be willing to make the sale, were it in his hands to do so."

Marden pulled himself up. So, she had heard him speaking with Alistair earlier. It explained quite a bit. It excused her in part, and still he was hurt. Pinpricks of fire set off his temper. He had thought she would know better. He had thought she would no more suspect him than she would Lara.

"I see, Miss Fernwood, that we do not understand one another as I had thought." He moved away from her, for part of him wanted to fly from the house. He could not. He thought perhaps that he might confide in her, tell her what he had been up to.

"Brandy . . ." He used her given name for the first time.

"I've got it!" cried Denny, reentering the conservatory and waving the emerald velvet thing at her.

Marden of a sudden decided what next should be done. "Denny, go and have a hot bath prepared for Miss Fernwood . . . and advise your sister that her friend has sustained an injury."

With this he returned to Brandy and began scooping her into his arms. She objected, and curtly he told her not to be a fool and would she please hold him so that they would not both topple over. She complied. In silence he took her upstairs, and she could not help but notice that his chest was solid, that his arms were well muscled, that his chin was well designed, and that she was totally comfortable and secure within his hold.

He put her on her bed, and she frowned. "And having played the gallant, you leave?"

He smiled at her. "I am returning with Sir Reginald, though . . . at your invitation, for dinner. Perhaps you should notify the cook."

"But . . . I cannot do that," she retorted.

"Then have Lara do it, for, my love, I intend to return."

With that he was gone. She heard them making her bath ready next door, and then Denny was dragging in Lara by the hand, who exclaimed fretfully when she saw Brandy's condition.

Marden made his way to the stables. Things had come to an ugly pass. Denny was not the only one now in danger. Brandy too could be a target. He stopped on a second thought and returned to the Spanish garden's walls and traveled its outer lengths, coming to a stop near the spot the now crushed urn had once occupied. In the brush below was a rusted iron crowbar. He picked it up. Someone had been waiting, watching Denny's progress through the crevices in the wall. . . .

But who? He had attempted to entrap Alistair this morning, but the man had not given himself away. He was either too clever to do so, or innocent. Could Alistair have come outside after their discussion? Had he seen Denny? Had he loosened the urn with the crowbar, sent it flying over the wall as Denny approached? Who else stood to gain?

There was Cynthia Hayward, Alistair's mother.

168

She might wish her son to be lord of Quendon. She would like that. Cynthia and the doctor were lovers . . . which might mean something. He had warned the doctor off this morning, but was the doctor a part of their schemes? Were mother and son working together?

And of course there was Deana Hopkins. Fair Deana. What could be her purpose in wanting Denny out of the way and Alistair as lord? It might benefit her in some obscure long-range manner, but enough to commit murder against a child?

And Lara? What of Lara? If Lara wanted Alistair and her home, murdering her brother would be a way to it. No. The girl had no pluck, no mien for such work. It was in fact a source of surprise that such as Brandy would be friend to Lara. They were so different.

How to trap this man . . . or woman? Denny was the bait, but could he control the situation? And Brandy . . . how it had singed his heart to find himself under suspicion. She had not given him the benefit of the doubt. She had lined him up with all the rest!

FIFTEEN

Lara twisted her handkerchief in her hands and eyed Brandy questioningly as they waited for Brandy's bath to be prepared.

"What . . . what exactly did happen?" She was almost afraid of what her friend would answer.

Brandy took a long breath of air and leveled an open look at her friend. "An urn . . . mysteriously came loose from the wall flanking the Spanish garden. Denny was right under it."

"Yes, yes, I know . . . he told me you saved him, pushed him out of the way and caught the brunt of it. Oh, Brandy . . ." She put an arm about her friend's waist and dropped a kiss on her forehead. "You have been more a sister to Denny these last few days than ever I have been. . . ."

"Nonsense. . . . Now, help me with my buttons, and then, Lara . . . you had best tell cook to expect guests to dinner."

"What?" ejaculated Lara in some surprise. "Who?"

"I expect Marden will return with Sir Reginald . . . and probably Fisk. She needn't fuss, something simple will do."

"What is going on? Why is Sir Reggie coming here?" She was flushing.

Brandy sighed. She was tired. "He is, you know, my cousin. No doubt Marden thought he might wish to see me . . . settle me down."

"Settle you down . . ." Her eyes grew wide. "Brandy . . . do you think this was contrived? Was that urn meant to fall on Denny? Brandy, tell me!"

"It is what I think. Lara . . . we are going to have to keep our eyes open. You are going to have to help me. I can't be everywhere."

"Yes . . . yes . . . you are right. I have been thinking only of myself. Pitying myself. Brandy . . . is it Alistair?"

"I don't know. He does stand to gain a great deal."

"So does Marden," said Lara.

"Marden does well enough without having to kill a child for a piece of land!" defended Brandy without thinking. It occurred to her that this was true, yet earlier, she had suspected him.

Lara undid the last of the buttons, and Brandy slipped out of her gown.

"You had best go tell cook about our guests," suggested Brandy.

"Oh dear . . . Cynthia and Deana will not be here tonight. They are promised to some friends. I

171

had even thought we might go with them . . . but now, of course . . ."

"Now, of course, we shall dine at home with my cousin and his friends," said Brandy on a hard note. "Buck up, girl. Sooner or later you must face up to it—*you love Reggie*."

Lara went to the door and then turned. "I have faced up to it, Brandy. That is what makes giving him up so very hard." Quietly she withdrew.

Brandy relaxed in her hot tub, went from there into her nightclothes, and slipped between the covers of her wide bed. She ached with a throbbing soreness. There was a swelling in her left shoulder, and already a black-and-blue mark was exhibiting itself. She felt suddenly too tired to cope with reality, and a deep sleep came to her rescue.

Nightmares will intrude at such times, and they did. She awoke with a start. Images floated still, but she shook them off resolutely. The room was dark, and she took a minute to remember, to fix her bearings. A flaming hearth crackled and gave off the only light in the dusky room. Someone, probably her maid, had built her a fire. Above the mantel shelf was the clock, and wondering at the dark, she glanced at it to see it was nearing six. She jumped out of bed.

Marden returned with Sir Reginald and Fisk to find Denny grumbling near the library fire. Lara sat with him and turned to greet her visitors with a shy welcome. What would she do? Brandy was still asleep upstairs and she did not like to wake her, but it was nearly dinnertime . . . and what would she do?

"Brandy is asleep," announced Denny after the amenities had been observed. This seemed a very dull group. Sir Reggie had retreated quietly to stand near the fire and watch Lara from the corner of his eye. Fisk was pouring himself a glass of sherry, and Marden was frowning.

"Is my cousin all right?" asked Reggie in some surprise. He had never known her to nap during the day.

"I think she is just tired. I don't want to wake her . . . make her dress for dinner. I can always send a tray up to her," said Lara, not looking at him.

"Dull sport without Brandy," commented Denny. "And it's not fair. She won't like it, you know . . . she won't like it at *all*. We should wake her."

"Denny's got a point," offered Fisk, nodding his head. He held out a glass of wine towards Marden. "Came to see her . . . if we leave without doing it . . . might take affront. Don't see why she should, for it's not our fault she's asleep . . . but there you are, that's Brandy all over."

"We could, you know . . . turn things about," said Marden thoughtfully.

"Oh . . . what mean you?" inquired Sir Reginald, tearing his eyes away from Lara.

"It might take some doing . . . and it might be some fun," added Marden. "Now . . . listen."

Abovestairs Brandy had slipped into her white
173

satin wrapper, lit the branch of candles at her bedside, and put on her slippers. Quickly a brush went through her long copper curls, and then a knock sounded at her bedroom door. She belted her wrapper around her body and went to pull her door open.

"Brandy, look . . . just look what we have brought you!" exclaimed Denny in excited glee.

Lara followed her brother, and both were already moving towards the window table to unburden themselves of their trays. At their backs a procession followed, all heavily laden with trays of covered delectables.

"Oh, Brandy . . ." said Lara breathlessly. "Do forgive us. I made some attempt to stop them . . . I said you needed your rest, but they insisted you would like this."

"What is going on?" exclaimed Brandy, wide-eyed.

"Hallo, cousin," said Sir Reginald, dropping a kiss on her forehead as he forged his way past her and dropped his load onto her bed.

"I'll handle this, Brandy!" announced Fisk, wagging a finger at Reg. "You can't do that. Off the bed, I say. Can't have a picnic on the bed. It has got to be on the floor. . . . Now, spread that near the fire. . . ."

Lord Marden directed two lackeys to do Fisk's bidding and then adroitly dropped a kiss on Brandy's nose, much in the manner of a brother. She could not help noting that the sensation it aroused was a great deal different than any a brother could produce. She looked into his aqua eyes and found herself at a loss. His black hair glinted in the firelight. His hands he had clasped behind his back. He was leaning into her, and she thought for a moment she might swoon with her dizziness.

"Hallo, sweetheart," he said on a low, all too familiar note.

She steeled herself against his charm and said between gritted teeth, "I am not your sweetheart."

"Ah, so you have told me once before," he answered, not in the least disturbed.

"Oblige me then, sir!" she snapped. Really, he was an arrogant, self-indulgent, self-assured, shameless rake!

"It is my desire to oblige you as best I can . . . if you will allow," he said in a low voice. His hand strayed to her cheek.

She felt herself burn. Had a spark from the fire bit at her cloth? Why was her body in flames? Her green eyes grew dark with a smoldering sensation she blushed to own. She turned away from him. Had to get away from him. The room was filled with the laughter of a festive group, yet they seemed all so distant. Their chuckles, Lara's giggles, all seemed so far away. Only Marden stood out. Only his voice came through. He wouldn't let her go, he wouldn't let her chuck the spell aside. He meant her to know the force of his power.

"Ah, sweetings, so cool to me still?"

She turned to find his aqua eyes, and they were almost her undoing. Denny came to her rescue, and for a moment she wasn't sure whether she was irritated with him for the interruption or glad of it.

"Well, what do you think, Brandy? Grand, isn't it?" He beamed.

"Very," she said softly and smiled at his excitement.

"Didn't want to have dinner downstairs without you . . . no sense in that," said the boy candidly. "Marden said—"

"Denny, your sister is calling you," pointed out Lord Marden.

Brandy turned to Marden as Denny dashed off to see to his sister's bidding. "This . . . this was your doing?"

"Does it meet with your approbation . . . this picnic?" he returned.

"You are very good at evasion. Don't you mean to answer my question?"

"It was my doing," he answered. His tone caressed, his eyes stroked her tenderly. "I wanted to please you. I wanted your lovely eyes to sparkle as they always have. I wanted you out of the dismals. You worried me this afternoon. . . ."

She dropped her head. "I was silly . . . very missish, and I am sorry for it. I was a bit shaken . . . but I am really much better now."

He picked her chin up, and for a moment he did not know how he could keep himself from bending down and kissing her lovely rosy lips. "I have never seen you missish . . . though silly is something you are . . . often enough." It was calculated to make her react, and she did.

"Silly?" She puckered at him. "I am never silly!"

His eyes cherished. "No, you are never that, but

176

then you won't allow me to tell you what you really are."

"And what is that?"

"My sweetheart," he said softly and led her to the feast that had been spread out on the blanket by the hearth.

Later that night when she lay in bed, stared at her ceiling, and recalled the evening, it was with a sense of bliss. Absurd, she told herself. You are allowing a rake to win your heart. He will end in hurting you. It is their way. He won't mean to, but he will. And still the pleasure of the evening scoffed at such conjectures.

Everyone had relaxed. Even Lara had joined the jesting. The atmosphere had been cozy, sweetly, peacefully pleasant. They sat around the fire and watched the flames as Fisk introduced one ballad after another.

She hadn't even realized that she was leaning back into Marden's chest. Or had she? It was then that she felt him bend his head, touch her hair, gently move it away as he brushed her neck with a kiss both soft and bewitching. Her flesh tingled with the thrill of it. She couldn't move. Her heartbeat increased rapidly, and she wanted to turn in his arms. She wanted him to kiss her mouth as he had done that night. . . .

And now he was gone and the evening was over. What was happening to her? She had met so many of his kind. Roués, libertines, rakes. Their skills lay in their charms. Their victories lay in the fact that they could be all too engaging. Was he one of them? Had she lost her heart to one of them?

SIXTEEN

With Denny's increasing strength came also his natural inclination to head serenely into mischief. He had been, after all, an active scamp of a lad, and now that he was feeling more fit, he was also feeling more restless.

He breakfasted with Brandy and his sister, did his studies as they asked, and then felt it was not asking too much to be allowed to go and play with Sarah's puppies. This was granted to him.

He glanced around as he stroked the wiggling red lovelies. No one about. He wouldn't be gone that long. Lara had said she was going to take the curricle into town . . . Brandy might join her. No one would even know. He scrambled to the arch that led to the woods outside the stone walls and sped through the thicket to the road.

He crossed the road and found the narrow wooded

path that would lead him to the gypsy camp. He had heard the servants talking about the camp. They would be leaving the area soon, and he wanted another look at the young trained bear, Ramus.

Deana allowed the gypsy to take her waist in his hands as he handed her down to the ground from the brightly painted caravan. Her business with the woman inside had been concluded. There was nothing here to keep her. She smoothed out the skirt of her shabby blue linen riding habit and moved to take up the reins of the roan Lara had been kind enough to acquire for her pleasure.

Denny saw Ramus playing with a gaily colored ball, and with a crow of delight he came crashing through the woods.

Deana's roan shied sideways in fright at the unexpected movement, and Denny caught himself short as he stopped and stared with some dismay at Deana Hopkins.

"Oh oh," he said softly to himself.

"Denny! What do you think you are doing here?" demanded the lady angrily. "Your sister will not be pleased if she finds out you are running about the countryside. Just look at you . . . you are filthy."

"Aw . . . I was just walking about and thought I'd have another look at Ramus." He shuffled his feet. He had never cared very much for Miss Hopkins. She wasn't even a real cousin.

Deana's eyes narrowed. "Well, I can understand

that. Perhaps I shouldn't say anything about this to your sister. It might upset her."

"You mean you won't tell?" He was surprised.

She patted his uncovered head. "No, I think this time I shall have to keep your secret, which means, Denny that you must not say you saw me...."

"Thanks! Can I go and see Ramus now?"

"Of course, child. Go enjoy yourself," she said, smiling. She watched him go out of view and retethered her horse. Again she went into the gypsy wagon she had just left, though her business this time took only a minute.

Cynthia's mauve velvet gown clung alluringly to her tall full figure as she moved down the hall to the library. Where was that niece of hers? She wanted Deana to run an errand for her in town.

She poked her head into the library and saw Lara and Brandy laughing over something or other, and she frowned.

"Have you seen Deana?" Cynthia asked on an impatient note.

"Earlier," said Brandy lightly. "She was taking her roan out."

"Drat!"

"Is something wrong, Aunt Cynthia?" asked Lara, getting nervous as she always did in her aunt's company.

"I wanted her to run into town for me and pick up this order from the chemist."

"I will go for you," offered Lara.

Cynthia smiled and condescended to enter the

room. "Oh, will you, child? How nice." She came forward and gave Lara her list.

"Perhaps you can also stop at my dressmaker and find out when she means to have my gown altered. I have been waiting for more than a week now."

"Yes, Aunt Cynthia," she said dully and stood watching as her aunt turned and left the room.

"Charming personality, your aunt," said Brandy dryly.

"You must not judge her harshly . . . she is not a happy woman."

"Lara, you are much too tolerant," said Brandy on an exasperated note.

Lara picked at the folds of her dark brown satin day gown. "Do you think your cousin will be visiting you today?"

"Reg? After last night I half expected him for breakfast this morning. You two looked as if you were floating in paradise," said Brandy archly.

Lara blushed. "I . . . I wanted to talk to him. . . ."

"Oh, Lara, I am so happy. You have decided to tell him what it is that you think is so terrible?"

"No, I wanted to tell him that . . . last night has changed nothing."

"Oh, Lara . . . I am so . . . so very disappointed in you. Go on, then. Do your errand for your aunt."

"You are angry with me?" Lara moved towards her friend. "Please, Brandy, don't hate me . . . I have such very good reasons."

"There is not a reason in the world you can give me that will satisfy. Now, go on . . . go to town . . . maybe you will meet Alistair on the way and allow him to woo you into marriage!" With this Brandy stalked off and returned to her room. Her peacock-blue morning gown floated around her as she plumped herself on her bed. She was all out of patience with her friend. Reg was bound to be badly hurt in this. Badly hurt.

Marden had business with one of his tenants early that morning. It was something he could have put off, or left to his agent to handle for him, but he wanted the time to clear his head. He wanted something to take his mind off Brandice Fernwood.

Just what are you going to do with her? You are a bachelor. You know what women are—don't you? You've seen what happened to your brother when he lost his heart. You know what a woman can do. But this one was different, he answered. So, she was different. You might tire of her. In time you will grow restless. Leave the maid be. 'Tis not your game to play with virgins.

He was due back at Marden Towers to meet with his man, and then he meant to ride to the Abbey. He cut through the woods and smiled to see how different the sylvan surroundings were becoming with their leaves falling and baring the trees. He could just make out some of the gypsy wagons through the clearing. He left them behind as he took the narrow path uphill, traversing and barreling through the trees at a trot. However, as he weaved, his horse stumbled onto his left fore and came up off. Marden frowned, dismounted, and took out his hoof pick from the leather satchel

182

he always carried attached to his saddle. He took up his gray's right leg, and sure enough found a stone wedged into a loose shoe. And then he heard her.

Leaves of gold, red, and russet brown fell, and with them came a thin brittle branch. Deana's roan heard the sound, saw the movement, and in some fright shied sharply to his left.

Deana gasped, screamed with fright, and then became furious with the poor animal. "Stupid!" she yelled, and the resounding force of her gloved hand came across the roan's neck. He side-passed in some agitation, and she became incensed and brought down her crop upon his head. He whirled with her, and it was a moment or so before she brought the poor animal under control.

Marden watched as she left the gypsy camp behind, as she took the path below his hill and made for the road that would take her to the Abbey. What was she up to? Whatever had she been doing at a gypsy camp? Odd, very odd.

Lara was driving the small curricle towards town. Her thoughts were racing, her mood once again miserable. Coming straight at her was Alistair Hayward. She sighed and wondered at herself. He was handsome, he was pleasant, he would make a comfortable husband . . . and he knew about her mother. He knew and never mentioned, he knew and it didn't matter. Of course it didn't matter . . . he had no political ambitions. He was her brother's agent. Why should it matter?

He tipped his hat to her. "Lara . . . you look lovely."

"Thank you, Alistair. Are you on the way to the Abbey?"

"No, I have business with some of our tenants. Perhaps I may stop by later. Will you be there this afternoon?"

"Oh yes. I am only running an errand for your mother. I'll be there for tea."

Deana brought her roan up on tight reins at the sight of Alistair bending towards Lara Quendon. She felt a sick rage twist at her gut.

"Hallo, you two," she called and walked her horse their way.

"Deana!" said Alistair. "Wherever did you come from?" He was surprised.

She bit her lip. She hadn't thought. She had seen them together. She had seen Alistair look as though he were flirting with Lara, and she had only known she had to interrupt.

"Oh . . . I was just riding . . . took a shortcut through the woods," she said breathlessly. "The trees are so lovely at this time of year."

"Yes, they are," agreed Lara. "Well, I must be off." She started her horse forward, leaving Deana alone with Alistair on the open road.

"What were you two talking about, Alistair?" Deana asked lightly. "You seemed much engrossed with the fair Lara."

He eyed her for a moment. She was looking radiant. Fresh in his mind was their recent intimacy. She had no rights to him, he had given her none. Still . . . there was no sense putting her back

184

up. "Lara means nothing to me, and well you know it, darling . . . but . . ."

"Oh yes, I know, she is a means to an end." Deana sighed. "But Alistair, if Denny is suffering from consumption . . ."

"Is that what you think?" He was looking at her curiously.

"It is what the doctor said," she answered slowly.

"That's right . . . that is what he said. However, Denny may yet prosper. Miss Fernwood has been taking such good care of him." His voice was dry.

"Things could change," she said carefully.

"But in the meantime I am in desperate need of a rich wife. I have a great many debts. . . ."

Deana looked at him sharply. "I see."

Brandy put down her book with a sigh. Being laid up with an aching shoulder had made her restless. There was just too much to think about, and she had not really been able to concentrate on Miss Radcliffe's gothic novel. There was Marden. No, must not think of him. There was Lara and Reggie. Frustrating to think about. There was Denny. Denny? Just where was the boy now?

She got up and moved to her door, slowly, for her shoulder had stiffened on her. Down the hall to the schoolroom.

"Denny?" A glance around the room told her that he was not there and probably had not been there for some time, as his fire had burned out. She put her hand to her hip and returned to her room for a white knit shawl, then sped down the

185

hall to the back stairs, past the conservatory, and outside.

The sun had just managed to find its way through the clouds. It was a fine September afternoon, warm, breezy, and scented with the richness of autumn. She crossed the lawns, taking a diagonal shortcut to the toolshed, where the red setter, Sarah, had taken up residence with her puppies.

"Denny?" she called and surveyed the place. Mother and pups were resting comfortably. Sarah picked up her head and wagged her tail without making any attempt to rise. The poor dear looked exhausted.

Brandy put both her hands to her trim waist and surveyed the grounds. Where had he gone?

Lara put her aunt's package from the chemist onto the seat, picked up the reins, and tooled the horse past the village traffic towards the main road. However, her progress was soon halted by a fair young man who put up his hand and softly called to her. He needn't have said a word. She had seen him, and there was no way that she could have urged her horse on. This feeling, she told herself, had to be conquered.

"Lara . . ." Sir Reginald put up his gloved hand and touched her fingers. "All alone?" There was something wrong. He could see her withdrawal in her eyes.

"Yes. . . . I am running an errand for my aunt," she said shyly. There was such intensity in his eyes. How could she part with him forever? It was worse now. In August when she had left she hadn't realized how dreadful the pain of separation could be. Now, now she knew.

"Why didn't Brandy accompany you?"

She smiled. "Her shoulder. I don't think the ride would have been comfortable for her, and besides . . . I don't mind the drive alone. 'Tis only seven miles to the Abbey."

"Yes, but there was talk this morning in town. . . ." said Reg.

"What talk?" She was surprised.

Fisk had come upon them at this point and put in when Reg would not have, "Indeed . . . it seems some of those scalawags at the gypsy camp decided to ogle one of the farmer's daughters. They didn't harm her but it has everyone very much incensed."

"Well . . . they shan't bother me," she said quietly. "Now I must go, for it will soon be lunch at the Abbey and Brandy will be expecting me."

"Lunch, you say?" inquired Fisk, turning to Reg. "I tell you what. Instead of going to the Towers, we can see Miss Lara home and take lunch with them up at the Abbey. Brandy will like that."

Reggie grinned. "A very good notion, Fisk old boy." He turned to Lara. "If the lady won't mind?"

What could she say? Demurely she agreed, and her heart beat furiously. What was she doing? Prolonging the agony, that was what.

Marden rode his gray down the Abbey drive. It was nearing luncheon, and if he managed an invitation he would have Brandy's company for

187

the remainder of the afternoon. This was absurd! He was behaving like a schoolboy in love. He had to collect himself. Love? It was for fools, and he never meant to be one of those. And then he saw Brandy.

She was gliding across the lawns, making for the stables. Her long copper curls were caught with the breeze and swayed away from her profile. Her peacock-blue day gown moved with the swing of her hips, and he halted his dapple gray in order to watch her traverse the park. A moment later he was trotting up to intercept her.

She looked up and saw him. Thank goodness he was here. He would know what to do. Then she chided herself for feeling this way.

"Good afternoon, my lord," she answered his greeting, and then, as lightly as she was able, "Did you happen to see Denny on your way up the drive?"

"No . . . can't you find him?" He frowned.

"I have looked everywhere . . . the toolshed . . . the stables . . . he doesn't seem to be about."

"Have you checked the household?"

"Deana just came in a little while ago and said she did not see him. Cynthia has been resting in her room all the morning, and Lara went off to town earlier . . . she should be back soon for lunch. But Denny is nowhere to be found."

"Fiend seize the child!" said Marden irritably. He could see that Brandy was worried, and he was incensed with Denny for putting her to so much trouble.

Quietly she answered, "My lord . . . that is just what I am afraid of."

He looked at her sharply and then quickly dismounted. He was standing over her, taking her ungloved fingers in his hand, taking up the shawl she had draped over her arm.

"First of all, put this back on. I don't want that shoulder of yours catching a chill."

"But . . ."

"And then wait for me. I'll just have one of the grooms see to my horse." With this he was gone.

A few moments later he had her hand and was leading her to the southwest field, down a thickly wooded path to the Abbey's freshwater stream.

"Where are we going?" she asked in some wonder.

"Time was when Denny could be found collecting frogs at the stream. Maybe he has decided to take up his old ways." He was grinning at her, trying to cheer her.

Denny picked his own path through the woods. He had been gone for nearly two hours, and he was sure from the position of the sun that lunch would soon be served at the Abbey. That was bad. They might be looking for him now, and they must not know he had been at the gypsy camp. Lara would be furious and it would end with confinement!

He dashed down the open road and then bent to fit between the rails of the wooden fence that separated Marden and Quendon land. Up through the southwest field and then once again through the thicket. The stream? He would have to find a shallow area, and if only he didn't slip on the rocks he could get back without getting wet.

Ah, he thought as he found just the right crossing spot. Balancing himself with his arms outstretched, he reached to lay his feet firmly on one rock and then another until he had made the twenty-foot passage to the other side. However, in his haste he did not see his receiving committee!

Brandy, arms folded with her shawl tucked in at her waist, brow up, lips pursed and cocked, eyes scolding. Marden, amused but ready to dole out a lecture, for the boy had put Brandy to some agitation and that he could not easily forgive.

Denny reached the other side, took a step, and looked up to find these interesting expressions, and he gulped, "Oh . . . hallo."

SEVENTEEN

Denny hadn't waited for the scold. Hastily he begged forgiveness, and Brandy was so relieved to have him back safe that readily she gave it. Marden, however, was determined that the lad be read a strong stricture, and this he did a good five minutes. Denny looked so contrite and so unhappy that when he answered Brandy's question about his disappearance with only a vague "Oh, I just was walking about in the woods" she felt inclined to leave it at that.

They returned to the house to find that Lara had arrived with Fisk and Reggie. Cynthia and Deana greeted them, and it was not long before they were enjoying lunch. Surprisingly enough, both Cynthia and Deana's moods seemed festive, and lunch turned out to be a bright occasion.

Thusly encouraged, Reggie took Lara aside and renewed his suit.

"Please, Lara . . . tell me you have reconsidered." He put her fingers to his lips.

She glanced around her, for although he had withdrawn with her to the conservatory the others were still not far away in the next room. "Reggie . . . do not . . ."

"You love me . . . say it!" he demanded.

She looked at him long. "I love you . . ." She put her fingers to his lips to still his words. "And that is why I cannot marry you."

"You are not making any sense."

"Reggie . . . if you love me . . . go away . . . now . . . and . . . please do not come back," she said on a tight note.

Sir Reginald stiffened. He made her a slight bow. She could be obstinate, but he had never before thought she could be cruel. Very well, so be it. He was tired of grovelling. His heart could stand no more.

"I bid you farewell, Miss Quendon." With this he left her, made his way into the library, and took up Cynthia Hayward's hand. "I thank you, madam, for your hospitality. I am afraid I must be leaving."

She was pleased enough. It looked as though things had gone badly between Lara and Sir Reginald. She had noticed this during lunch and it had served to brighten her mood. Now Alistair should have no trouble.

Fisk called out to his friend, "Eh . . . what's this? Leaving? Dash it, man . . . I haven't finished me port. Wait now . . . I say, Reg . . . hold up . . ." But Reggie had already taken up his hat and gloves and was on his way across the hall to the door Jeffreys was holding open for him.

Fisk turned to Marden. "The man has gone mad."

"Ay, we had best see to him," said Marden, moving to take up Brandy's hand. Lightly he kissed not her fingers, not her soft knuckles, but the throbbing pulse in her wrist. Scandalously he teased her with his eyes. "Well, sweet life, do you think you can manage to stay snug and safe while I am gone?"

"If I want to," she answered naughtily.

"Then please . . . for my sake, want to." He flicked her nose. "I don't know when I shall be back, but if you need me . . . send word to the house."

"Back? Are you going somewhere?" Her face fell.

"Yes, but not far."

So it was she watched them go and turned to find Lara racing across the room, the tears in her eyes, and Brandy sighed. She turned then to Denny and noticed that he was looking a bit fagged.

"Well, young lord . . . what would you say to a nice nap?"

"Aw . . . Brandy . . ."

"Just for an hour or so . . . no more."

He was feeling tired, and so he agreed without too much argument, and Brandy walked with him upstairs. She saw him to his room, where suddenly he turned and took her hand.

"Brandy . . . you are the best of good friends . . . almost better than Henry Clay, and he is my very best friend. . . ."

"Why, thank you, Denny." Brandy was touched.

"That's why . . . I can't lie to you . . . I just feel rotten."

"Lie to me . . . about what?"

"This morning . . . I wasn't just walking about in the woods. You see . . . I heard the gypsies were leaving tomorrow morning early, so . . . I wanted one more look at Ramus, the bear. . . ."

"So you went over to their camp?" Her brow was up. "Well, thank you for telling me, Denny."

He wanted to tell her everything, but he had promised Deana, and that wasn't his secret to give. So he left it at that and went inside to lie down.

Brandy was about to go to her room when Jeffreys appeared with a silver tray. On it rested a sealed envelope. She watched as he knocked on Lara's door.

"Go away," came Lara's reply.

The butler shrugged and started to return downstairs.

"Just a minute, Jeffreys. Is that a letter you have for Miss Quendon?"

"Yes, miss. It just arrived by special post."

"I'll take it to her. It might be important," said Brandy, taking the letter off its tray and returning to Lara's door. She didn't bother to knock and was relieved to find that Lara had not taken the time to bolt her door.

"Lara?" she called as she entered.

"Oh, Brandy . . . I can't talk now . . . I just can't."

"Good, because I don't want to. However, you did just get this letter. It has come all the way from London by special post and I thought you might want it."

Lara looked up, and Brandy was moved by the stains running down her pale cheek. "A . . . a letter?" She took it and froze. "Oh no . . . oh my heavens . . . no."

"What is it? What is wrong?" Brandy came to her and put a comforting arm around her, "Who is it from?"

Lara looked full into her eyes and cried, *"It's from my mother!"*

"Your mother? But Lara . . . your mother died five years ago!"

No . . . no, she did not. My father set it about that she had . . . because he was so ashamed. . . ."

"Lara . . . I want to help, but I simply do not understand."

"My mother . . . never loved my father. She was married to him when she was only sixteen . . . it was arranged by her parents . . . and they were never really happy." She sucked in a long gulp of air. "She was only thirty-one when Peter Marden ran away with her. . . ."

Brandy's lower lip dropped. For a full minute she could say nothing to this utterance, and then, "Peter Marden . . . related to Lord Marden . . . ?"

"Lord Marden's younger brother."

"I didn't know Marden had a brother. He never mentioned him," mused Brandy, struck on this point. "And five years ago . . . goodness, how old was this Peter Marden?"

"He was eight years younger than my mother . . . but he convinced her to run away with him, and they left for the continent."

So, that was why Lara held Lord Marden in such aversion. But it was ridiculous. Lara's mother had been a woman and Marden's brother had been a boy. There was a question in Brandy's mind as to just who the seducer was in that particular ploy.

"Well, Lara . . . it does happen, and you cannot withhold yourself from future happiness because of it."

"There is more," Lara said quietly.

"More?" said Brandy, opening her green eyes wide.

"My mother was not content with disrupting our lives and leaving it at that. Within a very short space of time we received news of her."

She took a moment to compose herself, and Brandy, out of curiosity, asked, "Lara . . . your father kept *you* informed?"

"He had no one else to talk to about it. He was so ashamed. . . ."

"And Denny?"

"That is just it. Denny never knew. He thinks our mother is dead."

"I see. . . . Right, then, go on."

"I have often mistrusted Marden because of this . . . mistrusted his friendship with Denny. I wondered if perhaps he wanted some revenge. . . ."

"What are you talking about?" Brandy's tone was sharp.

"Some months later Peter Marden was living with my mother in Switzerland. He fought a duel on her behalf with another Englishman, the Earl of Stanwick. Peter was killed, and my ... my mother stayed on in Switzerland with the earl. She is still his mistress today."

Brandy was taken aback. This did give Lord Marden good cause to despise the Quendon family. But he was not the sort to hold a grudge against the many for the action of one. He would not hold it against Denny that Lara's mother had whisked his young brother off to Switzerland and caused him to die in a duel. Would he?

She collected herself. "Lara ... has this kept you from accepting Reggie's suit?"

"Yes, of course. How could I marry Reggie? The scandal about my mother could ruin him, and besides, even if he could weather it, Denny could not."

"Denny will find out sooner or later. Shouldn't he be told so that he does not hear it in the cruelest manner possible ... from a stranger?"

"It is not something I know how to deal with."

"Open the letter, Lara," said Brandy after a moment's thought.

Lara's hand trembled as she broke the seal and unfolded the crisp ivory paper.

Dearest daughter,

I grieve for you. He was your father and

I know that you and my son Denny loved him very much. I would have written to you sooner, but I have only just received the news.

Lara, understand me. I know what you must think of me and am sorry for it. However, I am not sorry for the life I have led since I left your father. When I left you, you were over fifteen, a woman nearly . . . and of course I could not take Denny.

Your father did not allow any correspondence and perhaps he was right. I hope you will think better of it. I want to see you. I want to see my son.

Next month I shall be married to the Earl of Stanwick and residing in London, where I hope my son and my daughter may join us for a visit.

With love,

Your Mother

Deana slipped down the corridor to Denny's room and without knocking went within. She saw him resting fully dressed on his bed and called out, "Denny . . . are you awake?"

He sat up and in some surprise exclaimed, "Deana . . . what are you doing here?"

"Denny . . . I am in such a muddle . . . I wondered if you could help me."

"I dunno."

"This morning when I was visiting the fortune-teller I must have left my purse in her wagon. I wonder if you could ride over there and get it for me."

He frowned. "Well . . . I am not sure I should. . . ."

"I will stand buff for you, Denny, and you can ride my roan over there."

"Your roan?" Denny had been yearning to mount the animal. "Right, then. You say at the fortune-teller's wagon?"

"That's right." She smiled and watched him shrug into his shortcoat and take up his wool cap. "Go out the backstairs door, and Denny, don't say where you are going or why . . . I don't want anyone to know I was there this morning."

He frowned, for if Brandy met him he would be hard put to lie to her, but he agreed—it was the only gentlemanly thing to do. He knew the rules of chivalry even if he was only eleven years old.

Brandy left Lara to herself, for the girl had to digest this new problem, and she could only do that alone. She was glad for the time to herself, for she too had things she wanted to think about. A walk. That was just what she needed. She picked up her white wool shawl and went outdoors. She crossed the park, and as she neared the stables was thinking she might go in and turn Brown Sugar loose in the pastures when she saw Denny leading Deana's roan out.

"Why . . . the little devil!" she exclaimed out loud on a note of disbelief. She took a hurried step in his direction, but he was already mounting and heading his horse towards the woods.

She would have to rush if she was going to catch him, and to catch him and administer a lecture he would not soon forget was just what she intended. She dashed into the stables, took a lead, and hooked it onto her mare's halter. She brought the mare to a mounting block and scrambled onto her horse's back.

"Now, Brown Sugar . . . if only you will not take advantage . . ." She sent her mare into a rolling canter and followed Denny's trail.

She could just see his gray shortcoat as he weaved through the trees. She found trotting too uncomfortable and went from a jog to a canter and then back to a jog in her attempt to keep him in sight.

Denny was enjoying himself immensely. He charged through the trees and never once looked behind him. Brandy was short-winded as she hugged the horse's flanks and attempted to cut the distance between them, but she wasn't able to do more than keep him in sight.

It was with some consternation that she realized he was heading for the gypsy camp. "Brown Sugar . . . why is he going back there?"

Brown Sugar looked interested in the problem but had little to suggest, and as Brandy slowed her to a walk she witnessed enough to send a shiver of dread through her.

Denny had tethered his roan at the fortune-teller's wagon door and called for admittance. No one answered, and just as he turned around a dark, short, heavy gypsy smiled wide to exhibit many missing teeth. Denny backed away, and before the boy could shout the man's hand went over his mouth.

Brandy watched from the woods as the gypsy dragged the boy inside the wagon, and she slipped to the ground a moment later. What was going on? That man had forced Denny into the wagon. Why?

She tethered her mare to a nearby tree and quietly made her way down the slope to the wagon. The man came out of the wagon, and she planted herself on the ground. She would have to crawl underneath the wagon. All these wagons had latch doors in their floors. She could get to Denny without being observed if she crawled. A few moments later, she had lost her shawl and had dirtied her gown, but she had managed to get beneath the wagon, find its floor panel, and squeeze within. There against a far wall lay Denny, tied and gagged and big eyes wide. "Oh, Denny . . ." she cried.

EIGHTEEN

The heavyset, undersized gypsy took his woman aside. "Eh, Carmen . . . you will bid them goodbye . . . tell them we go to join up with our own tribe now . . . eh?"

She nodded and shuffled off. Rose pulled out of her bethrothed's arm and watched Carmen's progress. Those two would be leaving today. It was good; she hadn't liked them. She had been pleased to learn that Carmen and her husband, Roman, would not be leaving with them in the morning for South Wales.

The short gypsy, Roman, moved to his wagon, which stood apart from the gypsy caravan's circle, but as he approached he frowned. Something white and feminine caught his eye, and he shifted towards it purposefully. He bent and scooped it up. A woman's shawl? He glanced around, and at that moment Brown Sugar wagged her head up and down, and the movement above him in the woods caught his eye. With a sharp glance towards his wagon he pulled open its rear door and charged within!

Rose watched him bend and pick up the shawl. She watched him look about and saw the horse above. She watched him dive into his wagon and in some curiosity moved towards the fortune-teller's brightly painted caravan.

Brandy was bending over Denny, reaching for his gag, when the sound of a guttural curse brought her around sharply. Suddenly she was picked up by her hair and found her neck twisted around as a large greasy hand closed over her mouth.

Denny wriggled and kicked with his feet. Brandy, his Brandy, was being abused, and all because of him! He gurgled within the gag's confines. He growled, but he could scarcely be heard.

Rose saw Carmen and pressed herself against the wagon. Something was going on within, but she could not figure out what.

Carmen opened the door and gasped in some dismay to find her husband struggling with a young woman who was no doubt quality and could cause some trouble for them.

"Roman . . . who is she?"

"Blast it, woman, how should I know?"

Brandy found the man had some loose flesh on the inside of his palm and managed to take up just a scrap of it in her teeth, just enough to latch onto, and bit hard. He screamed, and she cried angrily, "Let us go!—Do you hear?"

His hand came whapping across her cheek, and she fell against the wagon's wall. Once again he had her by the hair and was stuffing her mouth with a soiled cloth. She nearly choked on it, so deeply did he shove it into her mouth.

Rose jumped back in some dismay. The voice . . . it had been strangely familiar. What was Roman doing? Was he abducting some young girl? Who was it? What should she do? If she spoke up her entire clan could be held responsible. What to do? What to do? The villagers would not go easy on them . . . not these villagers.

So it was that Rose stood back and watched Roman, with Carmen beside him, slowly, lumberously move out of the gypsy circle and take his prizes with him. She stood for a long time and then she knew. It had been that girl. The copper-haired girl who had twice helped her. She felt her heart sink. She could do naught. All of them might suffer for Roman's actions. She looked up and saw Brown Sugar at the top of the slope. What to do with the horse?

She climbed up the hill and undid Brown Sugar's lead. "Go on, mare . . . go . . . out of here!" She gave the mare's rump a swift rap and the mare lurched off.

Brown Sugar, though, was in no rush to go home. The woods were full of interesting things to nibble at, and something told her that perhaps she should wait for her mistress. She had seen her mistress go into the camp, therefore the horse assumed Brandy was near. She put her head down and began grazing.

204

Lara could stand it no more! Denny and Brandy were gone. Inquiry at the stables told her that Denny had taken off alone on Deana's roan and that a moment later Brandy without the favor of tack had gone after him. Dusk had settled in and they had not returned. Quickly she scribbled a note to Sir Reginald and sent it with a lackey. She had been awaiting its answer for near onto forty minutes now.

The library doors were flung open and Marden with Reginald and Fisk came striding into the room.

"What is this, Miss Quendon?" It was Marden, and his tone was sharp. "Where have Miss Fernwood and Denny gone off to?"

Lara wrung her hands together in some agitation, and Sir Reginald went to her at once. Cynthia Hayward moved uncomfortably on the sofa and said doubtfully, "I am certain you are making too much of this, Lara . . . but if you want Denny and your friend searched for, you should be sending word to Alistair."

"I don't know where Alistair is," whimpered Lara. Something told her that Denny was in trouble. An intuition, a feeling, and she was greatly affected.

Deana took a turn about the room and said offhandedly, "No doubt Denny is simply doing what all young boys do—finding mischief—and your friend is probably just looking for him." In truth she too wondered what had happened to Brandy Fernwood. She went to take a sitting position by her aunt and watched the flitting expressions pass over Marden's face. Here now was trouble. Marden was a dangerous man to deal with.

"Miss Quendon, perhaps we may start at the beginning," suggested Marden on a frown.

"Good place, that, though in truth Brandy don't take to beginnings. Rushes in like mad, that girl. Plucky chit. . . ."

"Fisk?" interrupted Sir Reginald sweetly.

"Aye?" returned Fisk.

"Take a damper," answered Sir Reginald on a growl.

Fisk started to retort to this, but Marden put up a hand. He was in no mood for their bickering. Something was wrong. He could feel it in his bones. Brandy would not worry everyone by staying out this late. She would have gotten word to them, of this he was certain.

"Fisk . . . you remain here with the women. See that they remain calm. Reg . . . I want you to ride over to some of Quendon's tenants . . . look for Alistair." In a darker, lower voice he said, "I want him found."

"And you, Kurt?" Reg asked as he started to follow Marden out of the room.

"I mean to find them, Reg, depend upon it," said Marden on a hard note.

Reggie took his horse from the lackey that held him outside the front doors. Marden took his, mounted, and rode down to the stables.

"Weaver?" called Marden.

The old groom appeared at the stable doors. "Aye, m'lord."

"Tell me what you can as quickly as you know how."

"Aye . . . well now . . . the young lord comes in and takes up Miss Deana's roan. Says she won't mind . . . tacks him up . . . off he goes. Miss . . . she comes charging in after him . . . takes her mare . . . no tack, mind . . . not her bridle . . . not her saddle . . . loops her lead onto her mare's halter and lopes off after the boy. More than that I don't know . . . 'cept . . . neither roan nor mare has come back, which be a good sign. . . ."

"Which direction did they take, Weaver?"

"Southwest woods," said the man thoughtfully.

Marden was quick to catch the look in the old man's eyes.

"What is it? You thought of something?"

"I dunno but that I could be wasting yer time, m'lord," he said doubtfully.

"Out with it, my man. What did you think of?"

"Well . . . that gypsy camp . . . ye can get to it through those woods. Don't have to take the road at all, you know . . . jest keep heading southwest. Could be the lad—"

"Thank you, Weaver." And Lord Marden was off.

Dark was settling in over the countryside. The moon was but a crescent and scarcely gave off enough light, but Carmen and Roman seemed pleased enough with the dark. Two old horses pulled their brightly painted caravan along the badly rutted road. They had taken a back road, avoiding the main pike, with good reason. At the back of their caravan a roan was in tow, and within, Denny and Brandy, tightly bound.

"That ... er ... lady ... she said she wanted that boy done in near her home. Wants his body found. ... How ye going to do it, love?" said Carmen as she picked her teeth with her fingernail.

He shook his head. "Drown him. How else can it look like an accident?"

"How far are we from his own land?"

"Four ... maybe five miles. We'll go jest a bit further."

"Whot about that mort?" she asked with narrowed eyes.

"That's a morsel. We'll fetch a pretty penny for that one, I'll warrant. Take her to Bristol where the big ships are. We'll get a buyer there ... no questions asked ... see if we don't."

"It's dangerous, Roman. ..."

"Naw ... no one will be looking for us. She said no one would even know she was sending him to us."

Carmen smiled. "Aye ... that's what she said."

Inside the wagon Brandy's shoulder pained dreadfully as she pulled herself along the floor towards Denny. They had only one chance, for the ropes binding her hands behind her back just would not give.

He watched her as she used the wall to get into a sitting position. He felt her move her back to him and knew she wanted him to get back to back. He wriggled until this was done.

She worked her fingers against the rope binding his wrists. If she could just loosen his ties enough . . . Her wrists were chafed and the continual rubbing wore some of her skin away. She could feel her blood ooze down her fingers, but she kept up her effort and finally she felt his wrists separate. His ropes had given.

They lurched as the caravan came to a stop. She could hear the gypsy, Roman, jump down from his perch. He was coming their way . . . he was entering the wagon. Both Denny and Brandy stiffened.

Brown Sugar! Marden could see the mare as she straightened to inspect him warily from her grazing spot in the woods. He could see the gypsy camp below. There was a huge campfire ablaze in its center, but they appeared nearly ready to move on. He walked his horse down the slope towards them. If Brown Sugar was here, then Brandy could not be far. Where was the roan? Just what was going on?

Rose saw Marden astride his dapple gray. She recognized him as the one who had met the copper-haired girl in the shop that day. They were undone. He had come in search of the girl. She went towards him, hoping to keep him apart from the men, hoping to avoid a disturbance.

He saw her, and his brow went up. He bent over his saddle and said in a hard tone, "I have come for the boy and Miss Fernwood. You will kindly send them out to me." He waited to see her reaction.

She grew puzzled. "The boy? I did not see him

here . . . but the woman you speak of . . . she was here . . . she has gone." She said it flatly, feeling sick at heart. This was not the way to repay a kindness.

"Really? Then why is her mare still grazing nearby?" His tone was cold,threatening.

She bit her lip. "Look . . . you must believe me. We knew nothing—"

"Spit it out at once! Where is she?" Marden felt a chill of cold fear prick at him. Brandy was in danger. He could feel it.

She started to apologize. "I am sorry . . . I was not sure . . .and I do not understand why they have taken her. It was Carmen . . . and her husband, Roman. They are not from our tribe. They left camp an hour ago . . . and there was a dark roan at the back of their wagon which they did not have before. . . ."

"Which direction did they take?"

"I went after them to see . . . just in case someone came looking for the girl. She had been kind to me. . . ."

"Well then, woman, what direction?" Marden was near to screaming.

"Do not worry. You will catch up to them. They took the back road towards Bristol, and their wagon was heavily loaded. They cannot have gone far. If you cut through the woods with your horse you can catch up to them in ten or fifteen minutes, for their road is badly rutted."

He didn't bother to thank her. They had Brandy. They had Denny, and God only knew what they meant to do with their prisoners. His gray

210

was fairly fresh, he could cover the distance between them, and so he set the gelding into a canter. It was a dangerous pace through the trees at that hour, but Marden did not give a thought to that.

Roman stuck his head into the caravan. He had to hold his lantern up in order to see. His squinted eyes could make out Brandy evidently in a faint on the floor. The boy was scrunched into a corner, still gagged, still bound at wrists and ankles. He grunted with satisfaction.

"Don't move, you two, or it will go badly for you." He spat at them threateningly and then closed the caravan door.

"Carmen . . . I go into the woods . . . I'll find the stream, eh, and then I will come for the boy."

"We are far enough from the campsite?"

"What do you care?" he hissed.

"Roman . . . they are not our tribe, but we are all gypsies. . . . If the boy is found near to the campsite . . . the authorities will detain them."

"Huh. They will be gone in the morning anyway . . . and besides, the boy won't be found maybe for a day or two. . . ."

"Roman . . . be careful."

He grunted again and strode into the woods flanking the caravan wagon. It was dark and he had left his lantern behind lest someone see his light. He couldn't take any chances. The girl had paid him well, but not well enough to hang! A bramble vine pricked at his leathery face and drew blood. He cursed beneath his breath and put a finger to his wound. In so doing he did not notice the large pointed rock directly in his path. His booted toe caught it awkwardly and he went sprawling forward and landed with a heavy thud.

He sat for a moment, a hand to his worn heart, before he hoisted himself onto his feet and moved in the direction he believed would lead him to the stream he required.

Denny threw the rope to one side of the wagon wall and undid the binding at his ankles. He pulled the gag out of his mouth and went to Brandy. It was very dark and he could scarcely see her form as he fumbled for her gag.

As he pulled out the dirty material she drew in breath and licked her dry lips. "All right, love . . . are you frightened?" she asked him.

"No," he lied. "Are you?"

"Of course not. Think those two fools can hold the likes of us? Tosh." She smiled in the darkness. "Now my wrists, Denny. . . ."

He worked her bindings, and a moment later she was free. However, they dove into their places as the wagon door opened. Denny didn't have time to pull on his gag, but he thrust his face into the corner and hoped it would not be noticed.

Carmen held up the lantern. "Eh . . . whot's this, you two?" There was something wrong. The boy had worked off his gag. "Got your mouthpiece in order, 'ave ye? Well not fer long." She climbed into the caravan and moved towards Denny.

"Run, Denny, run!" cried Brandy.

Denny scrambled past the woman. She caught

him by the scruff of his collar, and Denny brought his foot up wildly and gave her a brutal kick to her shin. She cried out in pain, and Denny was out of the caravan and running into the woods. If only he could get away and get some help for Brandy.

Brandy had jumped to her feet, and as the woman made to chase Denny she shoved her hard, and the two began to scuffle with one another.

Denny felt as though his lungs were going to burst, and suddenly there was Roman looming above him. He darted out of the man's way, but Roman was quick to lunge at him and catch up the boy's ankle, which brought Denny down hard.

Brandy was out of the wagon. Carmen dived at her, caught her skirt, and yanked hard enough to snap Brandy's neck roughly. Even so, Brandy got loose and would have run free had Roman not appeared with Denny at that moment. There was a knife to Denny's throat.

"You . . . stand or the boy bleeds now."

Brandy stood. She had to do something. What could she do?

Marden heard a guttural sound. It was a woman's cry of anger. And then he heard Brandy demand to be released. The sounds floated to him on the breeze. His poor gray was in a sweat, and he was himself exhausted from the weaving in and out, up and down, but it had brought him to Brandy.

He could see movement. There was a lantern on the ground . . . there was a gypsy man holding Denny . . . there was a woman coming up behind

Brandy . . . and there was only one thing to do. He sent his gray careening towards the gypsy holding Denny. The man's dark eyes opened wide as he saw the gray charging at him. He shoved Denny away and dashed for safety. Marden brought his horse up quickly, his gun was out of his cumberbund and leveled at Roman, and Brandy was running into his arms!

She was crying and laughing and explaining all at the same time. Denny was grinning, telling his own tale and telling the gypsy pair in firm accents just what fate awaited them for their criminal behavior and their brutal handling of Miss Fernwood.

Brandy did not even notice that she had allowed herself to remain in the crook of his arm while all this went on. She only knew that he had come.

"Can you level this gun at his head, my love? I mean to bind them and get them to Quendon Abbey, where a magistrate can be sent for to take them in hand."

She took the pistol from him. "Wouldn't you just rather I put a bullet in his head?"

"Bloodthirsty girl." He smiled and flicked her nose. "Well, if you like. . . ."

"No . . . please . . ." cried Carmen. "Have mercy!"

"Like the mercy you were going to show us?" demanded Brandy.

Marden was trussing them up. "That's right. I think you should end it now, love, then we won't have to bother worrying about anything more than the proper disposal of their bodies."

214

"No . . . no . . . it is not us you want . . . but the one from the Abbey," cried Carmen.

"And who is that?" asked Marden. He had baited them, and it had worked.

"She thought we did not know her . . . but after she made her . . . arrangement with us I went and discovered who she was," said Carmen.

"Be quiet!" ordered Roman.

"Can I shoot him now, Marden?" Brandy asked innocently, for she now saw what he was about.

"If they have nothing more to say we must assume the crime was theirs alone," said Marden.

"No, it was Deana Hopkins!" shouted Carmen.

"Why?" asked Marden.

"You will have to ask her," said Carmen.

Marden turned to Brandy. "I'll put them on their caravan horses and we'll lead them."

"Fine," said Brandy. "I can't get back to the Abbey fast enough, my lord."

Roman and Carmen were deposited in the Abbey stables, where they were guarded by an incensed groom. A stableboy was sent to town to bring back the local magistrate and some of his yeomen.

Marden, thus freed of one duty, took up Brandy's hand and put it to his lips. Not a complaint had he heard. Not a whimper. She was a treasure. He was kissing her fingertips when he noticed the blood on her wrists, and examining this he frowned. "You have been hurt."

She smiled wanly. She was tired now, and the prospect ahead made her very sad. " 'Tis naught."

"The girl has got bottom!" Denny beamed proudly as he joined them.

"Denny!" exclaimed Marden and Brandy in one voice.

He blushed. "What I mean is . . . she has got the pluck of a . . . I mean . . ."

"I rather think we know what you mean," said Marden.

"You didn't see her . . . she worked the ropes off even though her skin was gone from rubbing . . ."

Marden kissed the bruise just above the dried blood. When his eyes met hers he was all too aware that every nerve was alive, that his heart was beating furiously, and that he was fated to be forever moved by this spitfire.

"Ah, Brandy . . . you've brought me a new kind of wine, and I swear I don't think I could live without it."

Denny frowned at them and brought their attention around to him. "What I don't understand is Deana . . . why would she want me abducted?" Vaguely he was aware that he had been in danger. Its full consequences had not yet sunk in, though.

"That is what we are now going to find out," said Marden grimly. He turned to Brandy. "Do you mind putting off going to your room and washing up? I want you as you are now . . . I want the full impact to hit her. . . ."

She nodded, but the smile was gone from her face. She had been thinking about Deana. It was all so very dreadful and could only end badly.

When the library doors opened, Lara screeched and went diving at Denny to take him up in her arms. She bent to envelop him, and it was left to Marden and Brandy to watch Deana Hopkins.

The girl went into severe shock for a moment and could not move. Her hold on the sofa arm strengthened, and her free hand went to her mouth as she gasped. "Denny . . ." She whispered in disbelief.

Cynthia Hayward turned to watch her. All along she had known. She hadn't tried to stop her, because she knew if Deana succeeded Alistair would inherit. She had seen the first time Deana had slipped something into Denny's milk just before Lara took it up to him. Later she had smelled the glass, and there was the hint of something, an almost garlic aroma, which Cynthia knew was arsenic. She had said nothing. She knew herself as guilty as her niece, but her part no one would ever know. Even Franklin was gone. He had realized, of course, and she had begged him to say nothing. He had agreed. What would come of all this? What would come of this night?

Denny pulled out of his sister's arms and turned an accusing finger towards Deana. Marden frowned, for he had not wanted to be so blatant. He should have asked Denny to refrain, but it was too late.

"She did it!" shouted Denny in some anger. "She hired those gypsies to abduct me . . . but Brandy came . . . Brandy found me . . . and then they got Brandy too . . . but we had nearly escaped . . . they caught us again . . . and then Marden came!"

Deana stood up and backed away from the eyes. So many eyes, all looking at her. The room was beginning to swirl. "No . . . the boy doesn't know what he is saying. . . ."

"You sent me to that fortune teller . . . said I was to get your reticule . . . but you wanted them to abduct me. You did!" pursued Denny, outraged at her open lie. "You even told me to use your roan!"

Everything had gone wrong. Deana's senses were revolving scenes past in her mind. Wrong . . . what was wrong? Brandice Fernwood. She was the she-devil. It was her. She had come and ruined everything. She hated her. Hated her. A sudden screeching sound escaped Deana's lips as she lunged at Brandy's throat. Marden stepped between, and Deana fell backwards as he put up his thrusting hand.

Alistair, followed by Sir Reginald, entered the room at this moment, and Alistair cried in shocked horror, *"Deana!"*

She whirled around and with hands outstretched went towards him.

"Oh, Alistair . . . for you . . . I poisoned him for you . . . I . . . pushed the urn over with the crowbar . . . for you . . . they were supposed to take him away . . . finish him . . . you would inherit . . . and then you would marry me . . . Alistair . . . for you . . ." She was sobbing fully now and looked for the shelter of his arms.

In some disgust he pushed her away. "No . . . what are you saying?"

"But . . . but . . . it was for you . . ." she persisted. Why did he look at her like that? What was happening? Oh Lord . . . what was happening?

Cynthia Hayward found a tear rolling down her white cheek as she went to take her niece in her arms.

"There, there, child . . . never mind," soothed Cynthia as Deana retreated into another, safer realm.

EPILOGUE

Deana Hopkins suffered an emotional and nervous breakdown. She was sent at Quendon expense to a sanatorium which promised to care for her. Cynthia Hayward went to take up residence at the dower house, and her son continued at Quendon as agent. The gypsy couple were sentenced to prison.

In those busy days of heartache, Lara told Denny about his mother. He scoffed at her and curtly informed her that he was not a child. He had known about his mother for some years, and he had learned the hard way. Sir Reginald laughed to hear this and managed to convince Lara that he would make no attempt at politics unless she agreed to be his wife. She did, and so it was that Denny returned to Eton and Lara. and Brandy prepared to leave for London.

Marden made one of their party as they traveled to London. He was trying to keep himself in order. Brandy's aunt should be applied to, and until then there should be no talk of marriage between himself and his love. And then it happened that he could wait no longer.

Brandy had impatiently waited for him to come to the point, and when he did not, she decided that he needed a push. They were on the road to London and had stopped at a posting inn for tea and cakes. She did not enter the inn with the others but chose to wander off to the gardens. There she strolled, pensively surveying her surroundings.

It was not long before Marden came in search of her. She dazzled him. She stood with her copper curls beneath her chip bonnet. Her blue silk redingote alluringly fitted her form, and her green eyes looked up to invite. Dangerous, he thought. She is so dangerous.

"Brandy . . . don't you mean to join us for tea?"

She turned seductive green eyes on him. "No . . . I need to think."

He frowned, "What is wrong?"

"Oh . . . Sir Reginald's upcoming wedding is bound to make Aunt urge me to take Alverstoke's hand. After all . . . the man has been courting me for three seasons . . . and I did say I would try to choose someone this season."

"Nonsense," said Marden testily.

"It isn't," she said innocently. "I am one and twenty . . . and Aunt wants me neatly wedded and out of trouble."

221

"A wedding won't keep you out of trouble," he said dryly.

"It might. Alverstoke has a very good effect on me."

"He is too old," snapped Marden.

"But ever so . . . sophisticated . . . and he does have such a nice way about him . . ."

"He can't ride to save his life. No hands . . . no seat!"

"Oh well, then it cannot be Alverstoke. Let me think . . . ah yes . . . perhaps Cory? Now, he is a beautiful young man. . . ."

He took up her shoulders. "You'll not have anyone but me, sweetheart." With which he kissed her long and ardently.

When he allowed her to come up for air she answered softly, "That is a truth, my lord . . . I'd not have anyone but you."

Let COVENTRY Give You
A Little Old-Fashioned Romance

CLASSIC BESTSELLERS
from FAWCETT BOOKS